John Braine

The Two of Us

D1428391

Methuen

A Methuen Paperback

THE TWO OF US
ISBN 0 413 57370 2

First published in Great Britain 1984
by Methuen London Ltd
Copyright © 1984 by John Braine
This edition published 1985
by Methuen London Ltd
11 New Fetter Lane, London EC4P 4EE

Printed and bound in Great Britain
by Hunt Barnard Printing Ltd, Aylesbury, Bucks.

The quotation from 'The Two Of Us'
is reproduced by kind permission of
Rondor Music (London) Limited
and Delicate Music Limited.
Lyrics by Roger Hodgson and Richard Davies.

For my friends,
Ann and Royston Millmore

Tell me, where do we go? Tell me, where do we go from here?
In the wilderness that this loveliness brings?
Just as long as there's two of us, just as long as there's
two of us
I'll carry on.

SUPERTRAMP

Change is almost always fluid; rapidly fluid, or slowly fluid; but even major events in a human life do not make the overnight personality changes that they are too often said to make. Marriage, parenthood, the successful culmination of an enterprise, a severe punishment, a dreadful accident resulting in blindness, a frightening escape from danger, an exhilarating emotional experience, the unexpected report of a five-inch gun, a sudden view of something loathsome, the realization of a great major chord, an abrupt alteration in a human relationship – they all take time to be absorbed by the soul, no matter how infinitesimally brief a time they took in occurring or in being experienced. Only death itself causes that overnight change, but then of course there is no morning.

JOHN O'HARA

One

On the day of the Lendrick Mills Parade at the Grand Hotel, Charbury, in the last year of the Sixties and the last week of March, for once in the West Riding of Yorkshire spring had arrived at the appointed date and had settled down to hand out its special gift of a brisk euphoria. The warmth was spring warmth, the sun was bright but not brassy, the day wasn't a precursor of summer, but sure of its identity as a spring day and nothing else, well pleased with itself and with every right to be so.

The older buildings accepted the spring with gratitude: stone both absorbs and reflects the climate and, whatever its strict definition as a substance may be, is as sentient as trees are sentient. The neo-Gothic Town Hall, the neo-Baroque Wool Exchange and the aggressively solid but irresistibly light-hearted Grand Hotel with its purely ornamental balconies and profusion of delicate ironwork all reacted as unmistakably as the human beings in the city reacted. The new buildings which had sprung up around the end of the Fifties showed nothing. The only reactions of concrete to the seasons are to stain and to crumble: it's not only dead but never was alive. And the new buildings had no shape but were merely boxes, the three-dimensional applications of abstract theories – and not elegant or closely reasoned theories either. The Town Hall and the Wool Exchange and the Grand Hotel each had their own shape, their own individuality, because they each were, however imperfectly, the realization of dreams and aspirations which were not only decent and humane but not far short of noble.

What all of this means is that, lunching in the Alexandre

Room at the Grand Hotel, Robin Lendrick was, at two-thirty precisely, if not uproariously happy, far happier than she would have been if, as is usual in the North of England even at the end of March, winter had still obstinately been hanging on, with lambs huddling close to the ewe for warmth instead of gambolling, the sky sullen grey, and heavy topcoats and roaring fires still necessities. Of course the smoked salmon sandwiches and the Mouton Cadet – a dry white wine which paradoxically had all the softness of a good red Burgundy – helped; she wasn't a dedicated gourmet or wine *aficionado*, but she felt that she couldn't have asked for a better combination of tastes. The bread, too, was absolutely fresh.

The six tall windows of the Alexandre Room let in not only the sunlight – a sunlight which was becoming increasingly ebullient – but also, she could have sworn, the smell of open country, the exultation of the uplands. The three huge chandeliers overhead glistened, the cream and gold paintwork had been recently renewed and still had a high gloss on it. Despite its size – it held the one hundred and fifty guests at the Parade with ease – it still had a curious intimacy, a festive raffishness which was entirely Edwardian.

She wasn't thinking in a particularly ordered way as she sat there beside Charley Horsmordern, the new textile designer taken on, rather surprisingly, on the recommendation of Clive Lendrick's brother Donald. Charley was a small fizzy young man with curly black hair and a bony and harassed face and large grey eyes which were both tranquil and devouringly intense. The eyes were now studying the array of cold food and bottles on the buffet table and, Robin was certain, each of the thirty tables in the room and each of the one hundred and fifty guests. The eyes registered everything. The face, though nothing untoward was happening there, obviously wanted to be somewhere else and wanted to be somewhere else very badly.

The eyes now went to his full glass and were briefly startled: He drank the glass at two gulps, refilled it, turned to Robin and took the lapel of her dress between his fingers. 'Wild silk,' he said. 'Funny. Smooth but rough.' The eyes looked at her face – the skin darker than fair but golden rather than alive, the fair hair which she helped along but didn't touch up, the dark brown eyes with the faintest hint of hazel – with precisely the same expression that they'd had in looking around the room. 'The colour's right,' he said. 'You can't match your eyes exactly. So you go for a tinge somewhere of red. And other colours too, to give the brown a lift. Brown's a stupid word, though.'

He let his hand drop. The dress wasn't figure-clinging and Robin's breasts weren't over-assertive. His hands had held the lapel of her dress away from her body. But his face, as he turned away from her to look round the room again, for a split second reflected the fact that at forty-six she looked a good ten years younger without the help of facelifts, a battery of cosmetics or long sessions at beauty parlours and health farms.

She didn't find Charley sexually attractive, though he was always interesting to listen to. But it's always pleasing to be desired.

So at two thirty-two Robin's happiness was firmly established. She was only moderately diverted by the dozen male models now walking slowly around the room and threading their way between the tables: but to be moderately diverted was for her quite enough. She'd sipped her first glass of wine very slowly and would take her second glass equally slowly, and that would transport her perceptions as far as she wanted them to go, nowhere near inebriation but on a level agreeably above the mundane. Walking actually wasn't the right word for the way in which the male models moved. They hadn't to glide; they hadn't to mince; they hadn't to look as if they were ready to fight any man in the room, they hadn't to be too staid and dignified as if taking part in a ritual. The Parade was a trial run and it was imperative that it didn't take itself too seriously. Nevertheless, a modicum of quiet swagger was essential: the clothes they were wearing were for men who would only ask themselves if they liked them, not whether they could afford them.

And this, being professionals, they all managed to convey with an almost insolent ease. And there was a certain sparkle in the atmosphere: the reason for the Parade was, ultimately, profit, but it was a social occasion too. Robin looked at the model nearest to her through half-closed eyes: he had stopped at the bookseller, Norman Radstock's table, ostensibly for the people there to look at his suit more closely. Norman, his small, neat features momentarily a little disarranged, was grasping the lapels of the model's suit in the traditional way of the West Riding, where cloth not only has to be looked at but felt. The model was tall, broad-shouldered, dark-haired with a Beatle fringe, smoothly tanned, his youth and masculinity consciously on display, a hint of the gunfighter's menace in his stance. The way that Norman stroked the model's lapels, Robin recognized with amusement, was precisely the way in which Charley Horsmordern had stroked her lapels.

Charley's eyes followed hers. His mouth drew up, a savage sketch of a smile. 'Butch is how I'd describe that young man,' he said. 'They're all the same. Mass-produced. And too young. I told the agency to send at least a couple of older models.'

'Maybe there aren't any,' Robin said. 'Maybe they kill themselves after twenty-five.'

'You may have something there,' Charley said. 'What else do they have but youth, poor sods?'

'I expect they'll get by,' Robin said lightly. There was a hint of concern in Charley's voice: she wasn't in the mood for that kind of conversation.

'Who'll get by?' her husband asked, sitting beside her.

'The models,' Charley said. He looked again at Norman Radstock, who was now undoing the buttons on the model's sleeve. (He was pleased with himself for knowing the importance of this detail.) The model's face was impassive at

4

first glance, but at the second glance it was plain that he recognized that in the near future some sort of negotiations might begin.

Clive smiled, drained his glass of wine and poured himself another. His smile was open, full of goodwill, an expression which the large handsome face, surprisingly unlined for a man only two years short of fifty, broke into without effort or contrivance.

'As long as there are chaps like Norman around, they certainly will get by,' he said tolerantly. 'There was a time when he wouldn't say boo to a goose – or a gander, I should say.' He put his hand lightly on Robin's shoulder. 'We'd better mix a bit more, darling. And you're in demand too, Charley.' He put his other hand on Charley's shoulder. Charley rose immediately.

This was two thirty-five. Clive was in charge, unworried and cheerful, Robin ready to support him. There weren't any reserved tables at the Parade, much less any top tables. Clive had from the first firmly decided that the tone of the Parade must be casual. The right kind of people – and those who had a direct line to the right kind of people – had, so to speak, to be shown around the Lendrick Mills' new range of top-grade cloths without any fuss but with quiet pride. Naturally the *raison d'être* of the Parade was to sell the product on display, and he himself always bore in mind that if one were too casual, if one said take-it-or-leave-it too consistently, the customers left it, went away and didn't come back. But too high-pressured an approach, too hard a sell, gave customers in this part of the world the feeling of an attempt to intimidate, to make them an offer they couldn't refuse.

The Parade was also a public relations exercise, but low-keyed, a free lunch so amiably relaxed that no one would be unduly shocked afterwards to discover that there are no free lunches. Clive had selected the guests with great care. None of them was of the super rich and some of them had no connection with the wool trade either. But a sizeable minority

5

were, in the Yorkshire sense, 'warm' men, rich in a special way, the bedrock of their riches being solid collateral. Warm men never go broke and their estates are always larger than anyone, including their nearest and dearest, has expected them to be.

These were the ones Clive watched: where they led the others would follow. And already his instincts told him that he'd got it right. Of course the warm men weren't clapping or cheering or even smiling: he sometimes suspected that to quite a few of them any expression of pleasure was completely alien. Still, he was sure that they liked what they saw and that the message would be passed on.

Even after he'd realized this he still didn't slacken his grip on the event, didn't make the mistake of assuming that it would look after itself. And Robin was beside him; they were a team. Without trying they made it unmistakable who and what they were, the leaders. And that, though they didn't realize it, was one of the reasons why, at two thirty-eight, disturbance was going to begin. It would begin in a small way with Robin and then spread.

Although they weren't drunk, were functioning so fault-lessly, by two thirty-five they had reached that first stage of drunkenness which the Americans describe as feeling no pain. Not that anyone else in the room was; it was March 1969 and prices were climbing, but so were wages and dividends and credit was easy to come by (and so now were credit cards). And the notion of being free to do one's own thing was still delightfully enlivening – depending slightly upon what one's own thing was and upon whether one was doing it to someone else or having it done to oneself. The Sixties were still swinging and Robin and Clive, without making a song and dance about it, had taken full advantage of this. They were fundamentally decent people, they had a sense of duty, their standards were pre-war standards. Or, to be more accurate, World War II standards: when it came to the crunch they'd obey orders and hang on. Nevertheless, there were people in

6

the room who looked at the pair of them and felt with something not far from hatred that they were too damned pleased with themselves, that the way in which they dominated the gathering simply wasn't endurable.

Not that Clive and Robin didn't have plenty of friends. They entertained in some style, though not as much as they had before Clive's heart attack at Ruth Inglewood's flat in 1967. Since Clive's heart attack, Robin hadn't been as active in amateur dramatics as she had been previously, contenting herself with the occasional small part and a seat on the Management and Casting Committees.

To some extent she and Clive had made a strategic withdrawal. It had been in good order. No one, looking at Clive now, his pale blue eyes lively and clear and no hint of grey in his thick light brown hair or fatigue in his face, would have known how near his heart attack two years ago had brought him to death. He'd given up smoking and obeyed his doctor's orders about food, drink, exercise and rest implicitly and without any sort of complaint. He didn't let the memory of the heart attack overshadow his life. If ever in the small hours he woke up frightened, he was frightened not by the possibility of death itself, but of the living death of a stroke. But he was able to think of something else, to fall asleep again. He would have found living in constant fear as unendurable as wearing soiled linen.

He and Robin had always been alike physically and temperamentally – tall, fair, strongly-built, even-tempered. Since his heart attack they'd imperceptibly grown even more alike. They weren't stolid or phlegmatic or bovine: quite simply they were calm and where they wanted to be. Before the heart attack there'd been a stormy period, their marriage had been a turmoil in a fog. Now peace and order had been restored, an arrangement had been arrived at.

They weren't Mum and Dad, cosy together at the hearth with all passion spent. And the arrangement which had been arrived at wasn't exactly conventional. Neither would ever be type-cast. And even when old they'd always be exciting to the opposite sex (or, for that matter, some of their own): people always wanted to touch them, people didn't mind being touched·by them. And, which can't be explained, they always had a good smell: people always liked being near them.

And now all this had to be paid for. It was as if they were cruising in a Rolls (or let's say Clive's Mercedes) at seventy on the M1 on a fine day, the sunroof open and for once pleasant and tuneable songs on the radio, and a tyre blew out. What happened wasn't naturally, as spectacular as that, and it affected only Robin at first; but Clive – and others – were involved with startling rapidity. And it began as Robin caught sight of Clive's brother Donald signalling frantically across the room. She nudged Clive.

'You'd better mix with Donald first,' she said.

Clive turned. 'Christ, yes. He's waving like a drowning man. You carry on, love. I'll soon sort it out . . . ' He strolled away.

'I'm sure you will,' Robin said, wondering not for the first time why it was Clive, the cheerfully unperturbed,·who should have had the heart attack and not his brother Donald, who didn't just meet trouble halfway but ran twitching and screaming into its arms. Three years younger than Clive, Donald looked ten years older, his hair thinning almost daily and his face corroded by deep worry lines. Robin didn't concern herself unduly with what went on at Lendrick and Sons, but she couldn't fail to notice that recently it hadn't been taking much to trigger him into near hysterics and that she never seemed to see him when he wasn't chewing antacid tablets. She put him out of her mind firmly: he'd never change, but then neither would Clive. She took her powder-compact out of her handbag and inspected her face quickly. This was two thirty-seven.

And at two thirty-eight, as she rose from her chair, Norman Radstock, Ruth Inglewood's partner at the bookshop, advanced towards her, held his arms out wide, and kissed her on both cheeks.

'Dear sweet Robin! *Couldn't* go without having a word with you!' His voice, she noted, had grown more mannered of late, the thinning brown hair longer at the back, his cologne was applied more lavishly, his clothes more extravagant. Today he was wearing a lounge suite and collar and tie, but the shirt was dark blue, the tie white silk with a pattern of hearts, and the almost mauve double-breasted, chalk-striped suit was of 1930 gangster cut. He might just have got away with it, she thought, if he'd been twenty years younger and four inches taller.

'You're very dashing, Norman. I love your tie. Enjoy the Parade?'

'There's some *marvellous* fabrics there. Poetry. Absolute poetry. Some of them are *me*. Your new man's a genuis. Not afraid of colour.'

'Have a word with Clive. Anything you want at cost price.'

'Beyond a poor bookseller's pocket even then, darling Robin.' He glanced at his watch. 'Golly! And I've left poor Ruth holding the fort! *Ciao!*' He blew a kiss, turned, took three light steps away from Robin, and turned back to face her; it was almost a ballroom *chassé*. 'News, my dear. I nearly forgot.' He came nearer, lowered his voice to a stage whisper. 'Stephen's looking for a cottage in Hailton. Stephen Belgard. But you'll have heard. Naturally.' He flashed her a quick smile. It occurred to Robin that though his teeth – small, white and even – were his best feature, the speed and the malignancy of the smile seemed to make his face cave in.

'Why should I have heard?' she asked coldly. Her voice was steady but she felt her strength suddenly run out.

'Of course not, darling.' Norman said. His voice took on a conciliatory tone. 'You're a very happy and mature person. You've come to terms with reality. I've always admired you for that.' He grasped her hand.

'That's generous of you, Norman,' Robin said. 'Spoken like a true friend. You're really building me up. You do build people up, don't you, Norman? Being so strong yourself.'

He released her hand. The smile came out again, nervous now, trying to please, staying a little longer. 'No, no, Robin. Not me. I'm a tiny bright-eyed bunny rabbit that scuttles into its burrow when the men with guns and dogs come by . . . '

'That's remarkably honest of you, Norman,' Robin said. Someone else seemed to be choosing the words for her.

'I am what I am,' he said.

'You'll have to live with it,' she said. Out of the corner of her eye she saw him snatch a last glance at the male models. 'We mustn't hanker for what we can't have.'

Norman threw up his hand as if warding off a blow. 'Darling, we can all have our dreams.'

'Some of us can,' Robin said. Someone else was still choosing her words. She lowered her voice. 'Before you go I'll tell you something, Norman. It's very important.' She paused.

'You tell me, darling. I'll listen.'

Robin looked him up and down. 'That's a fucking awful outfit you're wearing,' she said, and turned and walked away from him without looking back.

It had started. Now she was feeling pain. Awake, she was seeing in her mind's eye Stephen Belgard's face – dark, saturnine, blue-chinned, with eyes which were always sizing up the terrain, looking for the high ground. She had been tranquil until she'd heard his name, it was nearly a year since she'd seen him last; he didn't even appear in her dreams. There was no place now in her life for all his energy and discontent. She didn't want to take the high ground, she never had felt that covering fire was protection enough. She didn't want to hear his harsh voice again – a harsh voice from the harsh world of TV, a world which was insanely prodigal and grindingly mean, fawningly effusive and contemptuously dismissive, a world which was barbaric, meretricious and essentially corrupt. Not that Stephen hadn't, against all the odds, hung on to a kind of integrity – though by now, she suspected, it was a bit frayed round the edges. But the voice that had insulted Norman Radstock so decisively had been

Stephen's, she'd used the techniques of Stephen's world, going straight for the groin. She had been justified in defending herself: he had, out of a rather unwholesome sense of mischief, wanted to upset her. But she could have given him as good as she'd got without breaking the rules of her world.

Which, she reminded herself as she stopped at Seth Lensholt's table, was where she chose to live. There wasn't much ecstasy in that world, but one was secure. Clive had had sticky moments at the mill – the worsted trade had had more downs than ups for a long time now. Yet he'd always emerged from near disaster smelling of roses and always would. For – that had been one of the reasons for her marrying him – he was lucky. And Donald, sucking Bisodol tablets, swallowing aspirin, and when things were really rough washing down tranquillisers with whisky and water, would see lawyers and accountants and officials and whoever had to be seen and would ferret hysterically through piles of contracts and letters and graphs and accounts. And in the end, so Clive would tell her, he would, almost in tears, announce that there was a very remote likelihood – absolutely no more than that, and frankly he'd just as soon throw in the sponge now and save them both further punishment – that there might be a way out of it. And he'd have spotted whatever there was in the contracts and letters and graphs and accounts which could be read to the advantage of Lendrick and Sons, and Clive would go to see the men who had the power – different men from the ones Donald saw, who were basically underling recorders – and once again it *wasn't* going to be clogs to clogs in two generations.

She was better informed about all this than she had ever been before Clive's heart attack. As she sat down beside Seth Lensholt she let Lendrick Mills fill her mind. Seth, a large square, dour-faced man, didn't get up – though he was robust for seventy-one his knees were increasingly stiff – but his grandson Colin jumped to his feet and smiled. 'You look younger every time I see you, Mrs Lendrick.'

'Cheeky bugger,' Seth Lensholt said fondly. He'd gone into the worsted trade as a half-timer – half the day at school, half the day at the mills – at the age of twelve, gone to France with the Duke of Yorks in 1916 and had left the Army in 1918, a Captain with MC and Bar. He'd been Captain Lensholt with no trace of a Yorkshire accent as he pushed his way upwards before the Second World War; but as his fingers had gone into more and bigger and juicier pies in textiles, he'd quietly forgotten having been an officer and a gentleman and become more a crusty Yorkshire character who wasn't ashamed of his origins. He was a director and a shareholder of Lendrick and Sons, which is why Robin had come to his table.

'He's charming,' Robin said. 'Makes a nice change in the West Riding.'

'Never mind about t'bloody charm,' Seth said. 'There's a damned sight too much talk about charm these days. Folk smiling all t'bloody time, even when there's nowt to smile about.' He pointed a surprisingly long, tapered finger at Colin. 'I never see that bugger look serious.'

Colin laughed genuinely. 'I'll scowl all the time if you like, Grandfather.'

'The way things are going, you'll be crying soon, never mind scowling. There's hard times coming.'

'There always are,' Robin said. 'And always will be in the worsted trade.' She glanced at Colin; his face was square like his grandfather's, the set of his mouth was the same, but they were as if of different species. It wasn't the age gap that mattered. It wasn't that Colin was stupid; he'd taken Petronella, her daughter, out once or twice, and she had in fact found him better company than Petronella had. But the old man was tougher, the old man was shrewder. She had better listen.

'The wool trade?' Seth said. He sipped what appeared to be a quadruple brandy and pulled out his cigar case. 'T'bloody foreigners are running rings all round us.'

'We're exporting to them,' Colin said.

'Luxury stuff,' Seth said. He took out a gold cigar-piercer. 'You're a director of Lendrick's, Robin. You get a salary and you've got that nice white car – Triumph Vitesse, isn't it? So, you tell me. Isn't high-grade worsted what you depend on? And where's your buyers here for that today?'

'We're flying the flag,' Robin said. 'Letting people know we're there.'

'Flying the flag in Charbury? Frankfurtinterstaff is the place to fly it.' He looked at a passing model sourly. 'Nice cloth, but an Englishman won't wear these colours. Too bloody many colours. Too bloody bright.'

'They're very subtle,' Robin said. 'And absolutely exclusive. And marvellously blended. You should talk to Charley Horsmordern.'

'I have done. And he's talked to me. Told me how he looks at leaves and flowers and the sky and God knows what, to get the right colour. He's all right, mind you. Queer as Dick's hatband, but a decent chap – '

'Queer?' Robin was startled, remembering Charley's hand upon her dress.

'Nay, not that sort of queer. Peculiar. Odd. Still, takes all sorts to make a world.' He pierced his cigar. 'As for him talking – figures are what talk to me.' He lit his cigar. 'This do today – it must have cost a packet.'

'It's tax-deductible, surely?' Colin asked.

'You still have to pay out the money. The best way to save money is not to spend it.'

Colin grinned. 'I heard you bought a Rolls-Royce once when you were flat broke.'

'Cheeky monkey!' Seth took a sip of his brandy. 'And look at this. Bloody Courvoisier. No need for that. Or good wine either. Most folks have no palates. The Rolls was different. Besides, I didn't buy it. T'dealer was a pal of mine. I borrowed it. Hardly had t'cash to pay for t'petrol. But it did wonders for my credit. Who'd believe a chap with a new Rolls was dead broke?'

'You survived,' Robin said. 'And things were worse then.'

'Were they? We knew where we were. And prices stayed constant.' His Yorkshire accent, Robin noticed with amusement, was beginning to slip. 'And people weren't spending money they hadn't got. And the government and the councils weren't spending other people's money like drunken sailors . . .'

He broke off. A couple at another table were smiling into a Press camera, the woman making a big production of it, the man obviously bored, his smile more a snarl.

'You see them, Robin?'

'Bruce and Tracy Kelvedon?'

Now it was coming back. Energy and violence were hammering at the door. Or was it like the sea bursting in? Bruce and Tracy had nothing to do with her or with Stephen and yet they were involved. She wanted to run out of the room, but looked attentively at Seth.

'She's got the money. American. Well, I don't need to tell you that.'

'They're Clive's friends, really.'

She felt that she was being bitchy, but didn't care.

'They're nobody's friends. They're trouble-makers. They've too bloody much to say for themselves.'

'They're shareholders,' Robin said mildly. 'They're entitled to their opinions.'

'He's damned clever, I admit. Too bloody clever. Goes on too bloody much about management structure and multi-faceted production flow and the peripheral approach – but he's after something very simple. And she's worse than him. And she's got the money.' He reverted to his Yorkshire accent. 'Mind what I say, love. Those two are none the worse for watching.'

'They know you're talking about them,' Robin said. 'They're very sharp.'

'Aye. They may well cut themselves.'

'That's wishful thinking, Grandfather,' Colin said. 'I don't think either of them is exactly impetuous.'

14

'You'll have to excuse me,' Robin said. 'I've got to be social.' Her head had begun to throb and the smell of Seth's Havana, rather surprisingly, made her long for a cigarette. Stephen wouldn't leave her mind and now her feelings about him weren't romantic, weren't in the least tender, had nothing to do with real love. She once had thought, towards the end of the affair, that she'd been like Hans Andersen's Little Mermaid – the price of her being given legs and feet to dance with the Prince had been unendurable agony. Walking on knives, she thought, as she moved smiling towards Charbury's Lord Mayor, who was, according to protocol, to be the first to go. But it wasn't even that right now, she admitted to herself as she shook the Lord Mayor's hand and tried to inject some warmth into the usual social chit-chat: that, after all, was romantic too, it had dignity.

What almost overcame her now was an explicit, sweaty and totally animal desire: if Stephen had been there at that moment she'd have dragged him off to the nearest broom cupboard. It had always been like that with Stephen: when one's really thirsty, she reflected moving from person to person, slightly varying the social phrases she'd used with the Lord Mayor, always greeting them by name and concluding with a vague invitation for them to drop in for a drink very soon, one doesn't bother with decanting the wine or get out the appropriate glasses. One drinks from the bottle, wipes one's mouth and belches unabashed.

She got round to Bruce and Tracy Kelvedon in due course, not thinking now of what Seth had said. They were a well turned-out couple in their early forties, he on the make, she having made it, both well pleased with themselves and each other. Bruce's mauve silk tie was too identical a match with the mauve silk handkerchief in the breast pocket of a light blue suit which was too shinily mohair, and Tracy's pale blue silk dress, though obviously from Paris, was a bit too fussy, and she was a bit too well groomed, a bit too deodorized. She found herself thinking – or rather once again

15

heard Stephen's harsh voice saying – that they didn't belong anywhere, that they were Hilton Hotel people, Heathrow people, nowhere people.

Bruce and his first wife, Vicky, had been neighbours once: but he hadn't belonged to Yorkshire then. And Bruce had divorced Vicky because of her affair with Clive and other good reasons – but she'd always felt that the real reason was that Vicky was too good for him.

But none of it had ever mattered. And the desperate physical longing began again halfway through her farewell – *You know your way to Tower House – ring me any time* . . . And she was off again, not actively unwell, but keeping going now through sheer willpower.

'Ring me at any time,' Bruce snorted. 'She might as well have said don't ring me, I'll ring you.'

'Yeah, it's a good old English let-out,' Tracy said. 'I ask people to call me, I tell them just when.'

'She's so sodding gracious,' Bruce said. 'And look at bloody Clive.'

Clive was saying something to a silver-haired man in a black blazer who was brandishing a clipboard at him, not angrily but despairingly. Clive looked calm and cheerful.

'He's worth looking at,' Tracy said. 'Knows who he is. There's a guy who never had an identity crisis.'

Clive made a few brief notes with a gold pencil on the clipboard and handed it back to the silver-haired man, who looked at it doubtfully for a moment. Then he smiled. The smile made his face look older than it had looked before.

'You can say that again,' Bruce said. Clive patted the silver-haired man on the shoulder and walked away springily.

'I don't like the way you look at him,' Tracy said. 'Or at his wife either.' There wasn't any emotion in her voice. 'You're too hungry, honey. You let it show.'

'I don't really know what you mean.'

'Want me to spell it out? You want to nail up his hide. He did play around with Vicky once . . . And he's a guy who's always had it made, and you're from the wrong side of the tracks. Keep it cool, that's all.' She took out a cigarette: he lit it for her with a gold Dunhill lighter. She put her hand on his.

'Always there with the lighter,' she said. 'Listen, hon. You be Mr Nice all the time. OK, you're bright, you got a hundred letters behind your name, you can make with the words like nobody's business. But it's no fucking good if your face is saying something different. He wasn't the only one played around with Vicky.'

'I don't care about that. It's just that neither of them really notices other people. Communications come through to them from a great distance. If at all.'

'Don't be too sure, honey. They're not dumb. And they're buddies with just about everybody who counts in this city. You saw Robin with Seth Lensholt just now, didn't you? Cosy as a pair of snakes.'

Bruce shrugged. 'So what? Doesn't mean a damned thing. The gelt is what that old shit cares about. There's no friendship in business.'

Tracy sighed. 'OK. I'm not saying different. But people stick together in this neck of the woods. And don't tell me that Seth Lensholt isn't a mite pissed off about Lendrick and Sons, because I know.'

'I think we'll need him.'

'Sure we'll need him. But it's like needing the Mafia. You bring them in and they make their hit, but how the hell do you get them out?'

'You're over-dramatizing things, darling. I don't want Clive killed. Just generally buggered up. Behind the eight-ball, as you'd say.'

'There's no percentage in that. It's about time you forgot bloody Vicky.'

'I told you. Leave her out of it. You're the one who matters now.'

'You'd better not forget it. She was a lush and an easy lay.

Period. Hell, let's lay it on the line. Why in Christ's name is it needling you so much now? Are you missing her?'

'God, no! You're absolutely everything that I want.' A completely vulnerable humanity invaded his face: it was as if a computer had started sneezing and coughing.

She squeezed his hand. 'Fine. Message in plain language received and understood.' She stubbed out her cigarette. Her voice changed suddenly. 'There's Donald,' she said.

Bruce rose, beckoned and smiled in the direction of Donald Lendrick, in one swift movement bringing Donald into the chair beside him within a minute as if he were landing a fish. 'Donald, we must have a quick word.'

Donald popped two white tablets into his mouth. 'What about?' He chewed as if he didn't like the taste.

'Perhaps you should get a bigger share of the action.' Bruce lowered his voice. 'I do have a *concrete* proposition. Remember?'

'I'm happy as I am.' Donald's tone was stiff.

'Why don't you and Linda dine with us tomorrow?'

Donald belched unhappily. 'God, I like that wine but it doesn't like me!' He took out his pocket dairy, opened it and looked at it as at a death warrant. 'I'm all booked up, Bruce.'

'Phone us soon then,' Tracy said. 'Real soon. We won't take no for an answer.'

'Yes, yes,' said Donald. 'We'll look forward to it. I'd better be going.'

He rose and scurried off, not seeming to be aware of where he was going.

'He doesn't trust us,' Bruce said. He permitted himself a low chuckle.

'He's dead right not to,' Tracy said. 'But pretty soon there's going to be nowhere else for him to go.' They sat quite still and silent for a moment, smiling at each other. They were well content, they'd climbed the first slope and reached the rest hut. They were, so they believed, in control of their own lives.

And that's how it was with everyone at the Lendrick Mills

18

Parade as it approached three o'clock. Even Donald, who hadn't been able to resist buttonholing the silver-haired man in the black blazer to make sure that Clive really had straightened things out, shared the illusion. And his wife Linda, middle-aged and looking as if she'd always been middle-aged, had numerous problems, first and foremost that the new dress she'd bought for the Parade was far too like Robin's but didn't do for her what it did for Robin. Still, she believed that she was in control.

And, of course, Clive had no doubts at all about being in control. His only problem was a minor one: he, like Robin, longed for a cigarette. It wasn't that his nerves were on edge, that everything hadn't gone smoothly, but he kept remembering coming to somewhere near Tell el Aqqaqur, not feeling pain so much as hearing it and how the Woodbine – an Export Woodbine, a big one – had tasted. He knew though that the craving would pass. It wasn't a question of willpower, but of who made the decisions.

Robin alone knew what the score was. As she went out of the Alexandre Room and down the steps into the lobby, she kept trying to fill her mind with the promise of ordinary and attainable comforts – a stinging cold shower, a huge fluffy towel, a freshly laundered cotton nightdress, the curtains drawn in the bedroom, the cool linen sheets and silence in the room and silence outside except maybe for children's voices and a dog barking. And she'd poise herself for sleep and there'd be no fear except the brief fear of having no fear of not waking, of being happy not to wake. Then the harsh voice would break in again and she'd be a hot naked body losing herself and hating herself as she found herself again, dragged into death and pain and yet exultantly alive. No one would have guessed her feelings as she walked briskly but without undue haste towards the lift for the basement car park. But when she got into her car she sat shaking for a full five minutes before she could summon up the strength to drive the six miles home.

Two

At the moment that Robin finally started up her car Stephen Belgard, some two hundred miles away in Surrey, was sitting at his typewriter writing an article which would in effect coolly and scientifically savage a certain TV writer. He was thoroughly enjoying himself, putting the boot in where he knew that it would hurt the most, but stopping a long way short of anything which could even remotely be shown to be libellous. The TV writer had successfully sued a national daily for libel some two years ago to the tune of £20,000 damages. And although the magazine which had commissioned Stephen's article had had a trouble-free record for the last ten years, he had since Dunkirk always found it safest to assume that everyone but him was not only thick as two planks but on the bottle into the bargain. What other explanation could there have been for that libel escaping the notice of the national daily's editorial staff and legal advisor?

Stephen smiled, stood up suddenly and began to pace round the room. There was something feral about his walk, but no suggestion of being caged. The large high-ceilinged room with the plain white walls, polished oak flooring and oatmeal carpet was his chosen territory. The large pine cupboard left of the fireplace contained virtually every known item of stationery in sufficient quantity to last him for the next twenty years: he not only never ran out of anything, but knew where everything was. And there were no out-of-date documents in the home office to the right of the fireplace and no books which he didn't absolutely need in the two white fitted bookcases. The small pine desk was clear except for his portable Olivetti, a black pen-tray with two gold Waterman pens on it, a small notebook, and a stack of quarto typing paper. Fourteen pages of typescript rested on top of the typing paper in exact alignment. The chair was a plain pine kitchen chair. He couldn't work sitting on anything more comfortable. There was a steel and leather reclining chair and a dark green studio couch, but he rarely used either. French windows opened out on to a back garden of nearly two acres and to the right there was a bay window and a window seat. Stephen always sat with his back to the French windows and avoided looking to his right. There were no souvenirs in the room, no mementoes, no bric-à-brac, no pictures, no flowers.

His wife came in with a tea-tray: he looked at her unseeingly, then put his fingers on his mouth, returned to his desk, banged out a sentence, pulled out the paper, added it to the typescript and handed the sheaf of paper over to her. She dropped herself into the armchair with a flourish of her long legs, the skirt of her expensively casual blue demin dress riding high, and absorbed herself in the typescript, flapping through it with a sub-editor's speed.

'Jesus, poor old Luke!' she said. 'You know what you're making him out to be? Not in so many words, of course . . . A psychopathic sadist.' She sipped her tea.

He laughed. 'I'm being all too generous. He would be if he had the nerve. Or the physical capability.'

Looking at those spectacular legs, the skirt now having ridden up to where the tops of her stockings would have been if she hadn't been wearing tights, a sudden lust overcame him. She had always been the archetypal popsie, she'd always show a bit too much legs and bosom and her hips would sway a bit too much; she was the dumb blonde who wasn't dumb and who didn't close her eyes and think of England, but kept her eyes open and encouraged him to further efforts. But just now, a year after the birth of their son, sex appeared to be on the ration. It wasn't that she'd turned frigid: she was simply too damned tired most of the time. Julian was bright and bouncingly healthy and he loved him with a frightening intensity, but the little sod never seemed to sleep. And Rona, the mother's help, a large earnest girl from Putney, was somehow off-putting.

She continued to look frowningly at the typescript. 'You *are* a shit, Stephen! That car accident wasn't the poor bugger's fault.'

Stephen grinned. 'I haven't said it was.'

'Not exactly. I don't know how you've done it, but I personally get the impression that just for once that night he wasn't pissed out of his mind but he had a monumental hangover and his passengers' foul and perverted antics were distracting him.'

'Not at all. I'm quoting from him, actually. It's in his book. He always was a lousy driver, anyway.' He shrugged. 'Not that I care. My point is that he's a lousy writer. He's overrated. Every bloody line of his plays qualifies for Pseud's Corner. And he keeps on being so Christ-like about his sufferings, waves of pain passing across his sensitive features.'

She put the typescript down. 'Agreed his Man of Sorrows act is rather hard to take, why the hell are you out to get him?'

'Why not? You're not exactly in love with him yourself, are you?'

'He's never been one of my favourite persons. He nearly drove me up the wall last time I worked with him. He's a better director than he is a playwright, and he's the world's worst director. Couldn't make out what on earth the damned play meant.'

'Among other things it meant that Western society is rotten to the core and its time there was a revolution.'

'I never got that message. Never got any message.'

Stephen sighed. 'Of course not. Because there were lots of jokes and pratfalls. When he went into TV sit-coms he left out the message. Or most of it. Got the audiences, got the respectful reviews . . .'

He left his chair and began to pace the room again.

'For Christ's sake, sit down!' she said sharply. 'And isn't it

23

about time you closed up the shop? You've been at it since the crack of dawn. I thought you were taking a day off.'

Stephen slumped on to the sofa, his body relaxed, his face tense. 'Look, Jean, I'm not just an executive. Believe it or not, I'm more than that. Much more than that – '

'Yes, you are much more than that. You're the muscle, aren't you? One of the heavy mob.'

'Love, this article is something just for me. I've got opinions about the medium, I'm in the medium – I express these opinions.'

'Fair enough. He was the blue-eyed boy with your lot once, though.'

'When he was with us. Not that I ever liked his brand of sit-com.'

'Who cares?' She rose, put the typescript on his desk and came over to sit beside him. 'You need a change. Why don't we go up to Yorkshire? I have connections there too, you know.'

'I'll see. I don't have occasion to visit it very much.'

'Your father and mother haven't seen Julian since the christening.'

'You know bloody well what they think of me. You know bloody well what my whole bloody family think of me. They hate my guts!'

'You're an easy man to hate. So damned awkward. Even when you're trying to be nice.' She put her hand on his knee. 'Which you don't try to be very often. I think that's what I liked the most about you when first I met you. You don't give a damn.'

'It's my divorce they can't get over. Funny, that. It isn't as if they believed in anything very much. They haven't got the brains. And my brother – God, what a boring slob he is! The last time I met him he talked all fucking night about driving his engine from Leeds to King's Cross. Christ, you'd have thought he'd pulled it all the way by his teeth!' He laughed. 'They're false, anyway. Blinding white.' He looked down, seeming somehow shamefaced. 'I'd have bought him some decent ones.'

'Maybe that's why he doesn't like you.' Her hand worked its way up his thigh. It was a thin but not bony hand, with long tapering fingers, surprisingly strong. She used clear varnish now and her nails weren't as long as they had been.

'Bloody typical!' Her hand paused and pressed gently. 'I'd have been over the moon if anyone had ever offered to help me. Not that I ever needed bridgework.'

'Julian's asleep for once. Rona's drifting around the nursery looking at Dr Spock from time to time in a bemused sort of way. Sod her anyway. Moronic little cow.'

Her hand slid up to his groin. He sighed, looking out into the garden: there was well over an acre of it, sleek and well tended. Home Counties garden for a Home Counties garden party, with a large Wendy House and a large summer-house and apple trees and pear trees and a conservatory at the front and a large stone potting-shed with a loft, large and solid enough to be converted into a guest-house. Daffodils and hyacinths and jonquils and jasmine were already in bloom and no doubt the other flowers would follow in due course, if not before their time: in Surrey winter never hung on. The garden ended at the bottom with a stand of pines and a high wooden fence. There were sycamores and beeches and oaks and bushes on the land beyond, which rose gently into sleek and well-tended fields. And beyond that, he thought – as well as he was able to think, since Jean's hand was moving quickly now – was sleek and well-tended Weybridge with its sleek and well-tended people. All was too bland, even the sky and the bright sun were self-satisfied – it was let's pretend country, the landscape and everything living on it was a board game for thoroughly nice bourgeois children. He moaned under Jean's hand, then it stopped and she grinned at him, sharing his pleasure.

'Shall I let the prisoner out?' She touched the zipper of his grey slacks. 'Have a real quickie?'

A memory hammered its way into his mind of a red dress yanked up to the waist, of the clump of hair darker than the fair gleaming hair above Robin's beseeching yet demanding face, of being caught up as in a cavalry charge. But wasn't that too neat a way to put it? Hadn't there rather been an eruption of savage horsemen from the stony hills, a descent of marauders? There hadn't been any sort of conscious planning before what had happened at Clive's forty-seventh birthday party some two years ago – only, so to speak, the brandishing of swords and spears in the circle of torches and the names of heroes and old battles shouted into a frosty stillness, defying the night.

But Jean was here now, and he was pulling her to her feet. 'In the bedroom,' he said. 'And not *too* damned quick.'

As it happened, it wasn't; it was a full hour later that, lying naked beside her on top of the coverlet of their big oak four-poster bed, he acknowledged lazily a complete contentment, even though the room wasn't his kind of room. He didn't much care for the grey and lilac floral wallpaper and the matching curtains, for a start; though Jean had already started redecoration. The house was nearly twice the size of their old house in Kensington, though less than half the price. He had looked forward to a less cluttered home, fewer material objects, more space; but somehow in the six months they'd been there, there was – it seemed to him – scarcely room to move about. And over half the double garage was crammed with pieces of furniture and an almost lunatic variety of objects: ornaments, rugs, kitchen equipment, crockery, pictures, power tools which he hadn't the faintest idea how to operate. With extreme care it was just possible to accommodate Jean's Hillman Estate; Stephen's Jaguar stayed outside.

Looking at her now he wasn't irritated by all this, wasn't even visited by the troublingly plausible fantasy of material objects in her vicinity actually breeding. He was here in Surrey in an undistinguished but spacious and solid house.

His bright and indefatigable fair-headed son was for once asleep. He didn't have a mortgage or an overdraft. The words that day had all flown through the air with the greatest of ease and he could honestly, the sun bright through the curtains now, think of himself as being free and, if he dared use the word, creative. Not that it was part of his job for Saxon TV to be a writer. He was an executive, he made decisions and took risks, and he never forgot that in commercial TV if the programmes didn't get the high ratings the company didn't get the high advertising revenue either. He'd let it filter through to the highest level at Saxon that he was taking the day off to think about various problems. He'd done this because it had filtered through to him from the highest level that they were irritated about losing Luke. He hadn't been ordered to write the article and he wouldn't bother to bring it to anyone's attention. If it achieved what was intended he wouldn't need to. He had to be patient and discreet but always apparently nonchalant and then in the not too distant future he'd coax the large organization he was part of in the direction he desired, like a tug bringing in the *Queen Elizabeth* or a mahout on his elephant.

And in the meantime there was the line of Jean's back as she lay half-asleep. He stroked from her nape to her buttocks, reflecting on the quality of the curve: he'd never really studied a man's naked back, but he knew it was different, even for an athlete. A woman's back sprung more, curved more smoothly, wasn't aggressive, but wasn't weakly submissive either.

Jean turned and sat up over him. 'I can't think what you want,' she said very softly. 'I'm sure there's time.'

'I was admiring you. The Rokeby Venus pose.'

'That's my favourite.' She touched her breasts. 'My boobs droop a bit now. Recumbent they're fine.'

'They're fine from any angle.' Before he'd finished speaking he detected the falseness in his words. As a normal man he meant them, as her husband he meant them: he was grown-up now, if anything the slackening of her body was for him synonymous with peace and comfort.

And so, he thought with a certain measure of self-loathing, is the peace and comfort of her not inconsiderable nest-egg – though it wasn't what I married her for – and her future earning capacity. And is this tree-lined Surrey cul-de-sac where I want to be? And why did I make enquiries about a cottage in Hailton?

Her hand busied itself at his groin. 'I wonder if I could make any changes?'

He forced a smile. 'Later, my love. I hear Rona shambling around, breaking everything in her path. I'm not so young as I used to be.'

'You're young enough for me.' She got out of bed and took down a towelling dressing-gown from the hook behind the door. 'Why don't we go up to Yorkshire? I do have relations there. Or used to have. They've gone away now.'

'People do go away from Yorkshire.'

'Some stay.' She looked at him sharply. 'Might you transfer there?'

'I could arrange it. The Chairman's dabbling in various things in the West Riding. He's a great dabbler.'

She took two cigarettes from the pack on the bedside table, lit them, and handed one to him.

'You know I can't dabble. I was an actress, now I'm a wife and mother.'

'No reason why you can't be all three.'

'Who knows?' She ruffled his hair. 'You're going grey. Just a bit. Doesn't matter. Rather suits you. But I don't like keeping too many balls in the air. It's tiring.'

'See how you feel. We'll get more help. You need a proper nanny, really.'

'I had a nanny. So I didn't have a mother. I'm going to be Julian's mother. No one else.'

'All right, honey. I'm not arguing.' He looked at his watch. 'I'd better have a shower. Haven't we got Ian and Tessa coming? Roland and Beverley too.' He snarled. 'A fun-packed evening.'

'They could be worse,' she said mildly. 'They are our neighbours. Try not to be too scintillating and scornful. They think they're being got at.'

'I'll pour on the charm.' He moved over to her and kissed her cheek. Her skin was very hot. 'We'll have a break soon. I'll fix something up about Yorkshire.'

'I'm positive you'll do just that,' she said. 'Into my heart an air that kills / From yon far country blows . . .' She ruffled his hair again. 'You think about Yorkshire a lot.'

'I rarely even talk about it,' he said.

'I know, Stephen. What does that prove?'

He shrugged. 'That's too clever for me.' He was trying to keep his tone light. 'You tell me.'

She turned to leave the room. 'In my own good time. But don't kid yourself, love. You can't be in two places at once.' She closed the door behind her very gently. He smiled to himself: she'd always been very good at exits, and that one – oblique, against the grain – was her best yet.

Three

The town of Hailton itself wasn't particularly in Stephen's mind when he thought of Robin. He saw her, he saw the hills around the town, he lifted his eyes up to the hills. Throstlehill, some four miles north of the town centre, was where Robin lived and where the moors began. He didn't see her in her home, he saw her on the moors. The ground rose steeply to Throstlehill, the road was narrow and winding, the walls and the buildings stone. It wasn't exactly a bleak landscape, but seemed well able to look after itself. It didn't try to please. The taste grew stronger and the air keener as the road climbed upwards, and beyond Throstlehill and its sheltering woods was the short springy grass, the drystone walls, and beyond the drystone walls no more walls, open country, space and solitude.

This is where he saw Robin. They'd be alone and there'd be a cool breeze. The colours would be dark green with patches of lighter green and there'd be the grey of the rocks and the sparkle of water from little streams on a bright day, which by a long stretch of the imagination could be described as silver. And there were the different shades of the sky and the different shades of the clouds and in summer the purple of the heather. And that was about the full extent of the palette. No more was needed because the variations were so subtle and yet so pure. The silence was subtle and pure also, and the sound of insects and the rustle of grass and the cry of the curlew and the distant bleating of sheep were integral parts of it. And there was the sweet smell of grass. Sweet wasn't the right word, but that was as near as he'd ever get to it.

31

What meant the most to him, however, was the certitude that on this stretch of moorland there was plenty of time, huge untapped deposits of the most precious kind of time: and he and Robin would own the exclusive rights. Strangely enough, he and Robin had never been on the moors together, nor indeed very often together even in others' company in Yorkshire in recent years. Their one encounter alone in Yorkshire had been at Clive's birthday party: the consummation had been prodigiously complete but there emphatically hadn't been plenty of time. The affair had run its course in London, and even there with an eye on the clock.

The picture he had of Robin and himself together had now come to stay, and in a drawer in his office were brochures from estate agents listing cottages in Hailton and district. He'd had the brochures sent to his office and he hadn't told Jean or anyone else, but one of the estate agents had been Hardrow's of Charbury, and the manager of Hardrow's was an acquaintance of Norman Radstock's. Four days before the Lendrick Mills Parade, over a casual drink at the Jolly Waggoner in Charbury, the manager, an amiable and easygoing man and a mainstay of the Charbury Little Theatre, had let drop his snippet of news about Stephen. A local man, he was mildly pleased about it. Stephen was a local man and when he'd been a TV face rather than a power behind the scenes, had been something of a celebrity. Norman received the news with due appreciation and went on to talk about the radio magazine programme he and the manager had just taken part in at the BBC studios nearby.

The manager knew nothing personally about Stephen, much less about Robin or Clive or Norman himself, or Ruth Inglewood. Norman left the Jolly Waggoner quietly happy and returned home to the flat he shared with Ruth. He kept his secret until after lunch at the Parade when he told Robin, and told it to Ruth some twenty minutes after his return from the Parade.

The shop was empty except for a tousle-haired young man

in jeans gloomily inspecting the history section, a typewritten list in his hand. It was generally busier than this; it was in what had always been the best position in the High Street and was the only bookshop in Hailton. But neither was disturbed: Ruth behind the cash desk was, in fact, glad of the opportunity to daydream for a while, and Norman, in the moment before he delivered his message, had glanced round the shop and had reflected with satisfaction that the new fitted maroon, green and red carpet looked twice what it had cost and effectively took off the institutional curse from the newly decorated white walls and ceiling and the predominantly white furniture and fittings.

He almost whispered his news.

'Say that again.' Ruth's eyes were wide open, her hand flew to her heart, she drew in her breath: her astonishment was too emphatic to be anything other than unfeigned.

'Stephen Belgard's looking for a cottage in Hailton. Or nearby.' He smiled: her reaction was not quite as gratifying as Robin's, but she wouldn't want to hit out at him either.

'I honestly don't believe it. He's got a wife, he's got a young child. There'll be no end of trouble – '

'You know me, darling. My information's absolutely reliable.'

'I know you all right.' The look in the sea-green eyes was now one of reluctant admiration. 'Sometimes I think you have the whole bloody West Riding bugged.'

'I keep my eyes and ears open.'

'Yes,' she said, with a warning glance at the tousle-haired young man in the history section. 'And a lot of other people in Hailton do.'

'There isn't any reason why he shouldn't want a weekend place somewhere on the moors. He is a local lad, after all.'

'Not a Hailton lad. But why not the Dales? Why not somewhere in the region of Skipton, or Settle, or Thirsk?'

'That's a rhetorical question, isn't it? Maybe cottages are cheaper round here.'

'Like hell they are! Not that I suppose that bothers him.' They were keeping the tone neutral and their voices low, but tension was building up. There was concern in her expression, and it was a concern which was not for herself: and his face was being taken over by the naughtiness of a small boy, a cruel, snub-nosed small boy, fastening a fire-cracker to a puppy's tail.

'I've heard he's doing terribly, terribly well. Power-hungry and power-mad, a real media Machiavelli. Going up fast. Not just a pretty face any more.'

'I'm not *au courant* with these things, Norman. It seems pretty odd to me, that's all – '

She broke off as the tousle-headed young man approached the cash desk with half a dozen paperbacks, smiled at him, dealt with his Barclaycard and wrapped the books with automatic precision. The young man, his gloom exchanged by a positive elation as he looked at her shining chestnut hair and large firm breasts, bounced rather than walked into the High Street, drooping into a shuffle as he closed the shop door behind him and looked at his list again. Ruth slammed down the Barclaycard slip and glared at Norman.

'You've known about this sod Belgard coming up here for some time now, haven't you?'

Norman smiled. 'Not all that long, love.' He inspected his gleaming nails. 'Anyway, why are you in such a tizwiz? It's no skin off your nose.'

'Norman, what the hell's got into you? You're just stirring for the pleasure of stirring. Why in Christ's name didn't you tell me before?' Her anger was visibly mounting. 'And why tell me now? It's not a good moment, is it?'

Norman looked away from her. 'If you don't mind, I've some work to do. Dull but essential, dear. Keeping track of the pounds, shillings and pence.' He turned in the direction of the passage which led to the office at the back.

'The accounts will keep. You're not going to have long on them, anyway.'

34

'Have you considered that you're not being very reasonable? Or very fair?'

'You've known me for six years, Norman. And lived with me for five years – '

'Not really lived with, dear.' His tone was mild.

'Oh hell, don't play with words! You don't have any illusions about me, that's what I'm saying. I don't give a damn about being reasonable. Or fair. *You're* not being reasonable or fair. You're making mischief. However you found out about it, you should have kept your big mouth shut.'

'What on earth am I doing wrong?' His voice became shrill. 'I can't help what bloody Stephen Belgard does. If he does get a cottage here, do you think it won't be all over Hailton as soon as he sets foot in the place?'

She lit a cigarette and puffed at it furiously. 'It's no use you making a great show of washing your hands. It doesn't take me in, Norman. You've told Robin. Because, of course, you were bound to see her today.'

'You're too clever for me, dear. Much too clever and intuitive for poor old Norman. In my innocence I presumed that Belgard taking a cottage here wouldn't be news to her.'

'Why did you tell her, then?' She spat out the words. 'Were you just making polite conversation? Or were you at a loss to think of anything else to say?'

He smiled weakly. 'Darling, I'm always bubbling with merry chat.'

'It's not so merry any more, Norman.'

He put his hand on hers, a rare gesture for him. 'Darling, it was casual. Absolutely offhand. I'm very fond of Robin. And of Clive. And I love you. Very dearly.' There was genuine warmth in his last words.

'In your fashion,' she said in a tired voice. 'I suppose it means different things to different people.' She stared past Norman into the High Street; the sun was not as bright now. 'Why don't you go? The accounts will keep.'

Two middle-aged women drifted in, then three schoolgirls, chattering resentfully about the hellishness of mock O levels. Norman glanced at them, then back at Ruth.

'Are you sure you can manage?'

'Just go,' she said. 'I'm bothered about Clive.'

He raised his eyebrows. 'You people . . . ' he began, then stopped. 'As long as you're sure, darling.' He blew her a kiss and then walked out jauntily, *en route* to the delicatessen and off-licence to select the materials of a supper for two at his friend Gary's flat in Walker's Court off Station Road, not far from the High Street. It would be after midnight when he got home and, though he'd be quite sober, he'd be uplifted, talking a little wildly, outside himself and not quite certain whether he'd find his way back. For he would have been absolutely, unremittingly in the world where she – and Clive and Robin – were *you people*. He had been about to say *You people are unbelievable.*

He'd only begun to speak in this way since he'd met Gary, and she was beginning to dislike it. During the past five years a delicate balance had been arrived at between them which was nevertheless marvellously supportive, and now it was threatened. But she was suddenly too busy coping charmingly but efficiently with the two middle-aged women and the three schoolgirls – all wanting attention at once – to get to grips with the problem until she'd been sitting for some ten minutes with Clive in the White Rose, the small pub next door to the bookshop.

When she was with Clive she was actually able to get to grips with worse problems than Norman's funny little sayings, she thought with gratitude. Clive kept on an even keel; he always rode out the storm.

'You're quiet,' he said without reproach. 'A long hard day?'

'It could have been worse. A last-minute rush of business. And Norman was a bit tiresome.' She finished her gin and tonic. 'I feel better now.'

'Me too.' He squeezed her hand. 'I feel at home here.' He

looked around the small bar with the new red plush booths, blue and green carpet and new oak panels. 'I don't even mind them having it tarted up.'

'I thought you didn't like change.'

'Sometimes you've got to like it. Adapt or die. That's what's wrong with the worsted trade. Some of them live in a dream world . . . ' He looked at her empty glass. 'Same again?'

She nodded and smiled: he went to the bar and, though the barman was nowhere in sight, in a second he was there and it seemed that within less than thirty seconds she had another gin and tonic and Clive another large Scotch and both their glasses half-filled with ice, the way they liked it.

'You always get good service,' she said. 'You don't even appear to try.'

He grinned. 'It's because I'm such a big hulking bugger,' he said. 'They're frightened I'll turn nasty.'

'No,' she said. 'They like you. You give the place tone.'

'Not as much as I would have once. Threadbare upholstery and a yellow ceiling. Should have been white.' He looked round the room again: a middle-aged man in a blue shadow-striped worsted suit of what was recognizably to Clive by the drape certainly of the finest grade – the highest count of threads, definitely in the Super Seventies – puffed a cheroot and examined complacently a sheaf of papers from a new leather briefcase, and two young married couples discussed in carrying voices the shortcomings of *au pairs*. Ruth inclined her gaze towards the two couples.

'Status demonstrators,' she said. 'Holidays are the next subject.'

'They all try so hard these days,' he said, disgruntled. 'Never used to bother once. Not here, anyway. No one here actually smelling or stinking on the floor. But it was – oh, comfortable. Respectable characters getting gently pissed and letting the world go by . . . Christ, I'm getting old!'

'You're not, my love. You're a bit tired, that's all.'

He grinned at her. 'If it were tomorrow evening, I'd soon

show you that I wasn't.' He stroked the sleeve of her green velvet jacket. 'You always agitate me. Very pleasantly.'

'That goes for me.' She took a packet of cigarettes and a gold lighter from her bag. 'Clive, everything's fine with me. I'll always manage.' She opened the cigarette packet, stared at it and put it down, then took up the lighter, clutching it tightly. 'You're going to the Civic Society Ball tonight?'

'Can't get out of it. Wish I could. I've had enough socializing for one day. My stock of charm is running low.' He parodied a host's smile. 'I'm very good at flying the flag, but by this stage in the day I suspect the ship is beginning to sink.'

'I'm sure that Lendrick Mills isn't sinking,' she said. 'You'll both sail on into harbour.' She put the lighter down and picked up the cigarette packet again. 'How was Robin?'

'A bit tired towards the end, but so was I. I suppose she was making the best of it. She's damned good with people. Always has been.' He took the cigarette packet from her and extracted a cigarette. 'Smoke it, darling.' He lit it for her. 'Jesus, I get so tired of people not smoking for my sake. Do you think everyone's going to give up?'

'All right.' She smiled. 'But I will give up, you know, I really will.'

'It's not cigarettes you've got on your mind. It's Robin.'

'Norman, really. And – ' she assumed Norman's voice with an uncanny accuracy – 'You people. You people are *unbelievable*. Not that he said it this time. But he does say it.'

'Yes. I'm fully with you. Yes, we people *are* unbelievable. We take all the flak, don't we, love? We keep the human race going, for one thing. And do most of the world's work. But what's with Norman? What the hell's he to do with us, anyway?'

'He has a lot to do with me. We've shared a lot. Perhaps he's just a bad habit, but there it is.'

'Love, you needn't justify yourself. Not to me. Christ, I'm fond of Norman myself in a weird way. I've got used to him being there. He's like some hideous ornament one can't bear to throw out. The human equivalent of a Present from Blackpool.'

She giggled. 'He'd be charmed to hear you say that.'

'I always thought he was a happy little soul. Seemed happy enough at the Parade. His hot eyes were devouring the male models. Mind, I don't think anything came of it. My opinion is he was just window-shopping.'

'I'm sure of that, love. He's dining with Gary tonight.'

'Gary?' He grimaced. 'He'd have been better off with the male models. Gary's a really grasping little sod.'

'I don't like him either . . . ' She hesitated. 'Norman told me something. I didn't really like the way he told me.'

'I presume not about Gary,' he said. 'And nothing to give me joy.'

'Stephen Belgard's looking for a cottage here.'

'It might have been expected,' he said. 'There's nothing we can do.'

'I had expected you to show rather more reaction.' Her tone was momentarily chilly.

'I honestly don't care any more. Nothing I can do about it. I just march through the mud at a steady pace and hope to God my boots won't start leaking. I'm certain the next battle will be as big a ball-up as the last one.'

He didn't seem to be speaking to her, she thought, or indeed to be with anyone. She hadn't heard him speak like that before and she didn't know how to answer him. She was closer than she ever had been to him, for he wouldn't, she was certain, talk like this to anyone else. But she was also farther away than she had ever been.

'I thought we had won a battle,' she said gently. 'Some time ago. I thought we were going to win the next battle.'

He was silent for a moment. 'We? We don't have anything to do with it. We do the marching and we do the fighting. We don't plan the battles. If they do go wrong – then what the hell, back to the old drawing-board.'

'You're mixing metaphors.'

He looked at his drink. He'd only had one sip. She knew that he would now have only one other sip, a token sip. He had the ability to stop drinking well in advance of having had enough: it was like a safety cut-out, a sort of dead man's handle.

'We old soldiers do mix metaphors. We're a rough-and-ready lot. Stephen's an old soldier but he's not rough-and-ready. At least, he was at Dunkirk. Monty was in France in 1940, did you know?'

'Oh hell, Clive, give it a rest! Who cares about the War? And don't give me that rough-and-ready stuff.'

'Maybe we unbelievable people *are* rough-and-ready. Norman's told Robin, hasn't he? That's what you're trying to get round to.'

'That's it.' He had understood, and felicity had arrived – and rough-and-ready felicity, but to be welcomed nevertheless.

'You build something up,' he said, 'and then someone pulls it down. So you build it up again. *We* did, really.'

'Yes, we did,' she said gently. The felicity was still with her and what she was remembering now was the time before they were lovers, when Clive had been simply a tall, good-looking man who had discovered the pleasures of reading in middle age and who didn't have any inhibitions one way or the other. He didn't have any cultural pretensions but he wasn't afraid of Virginia Woolf either. They had been friends, they'd liked each other as persons, they'd liked each other's company from the first.

'We built it up again,' he said. 'It suits us, doesn't it?' He rubbed his eyes. 'I wonder how Norman got the news.'

'Don't ask me, darling. He gets around quite a bit.'

'A bit too bloody much,' he said sourly. 'He really is stirring it.'

She looked at him with concern. The felicity was still with her and would carry her through, but this wasn't Clive. 'He might have got the wrong story.'

40

He seemed not to hear, then took another sip of whisky. 'Yes, you're right,' he said, looking at the two young married couples. 'They really are status demonstrators. And into holidays now. Kenya was mentioned. And Fiji . . . ' He hadn't bothered to lower his voice. One young man turned his head to look at Clive, not having taken in his words, but sensing aggression.

Ruth stood up. 'Let's go, darling,' she said.

Clive looked towards the two young married couples rather amusedly, then stood up and followed her to the door.

'What got into you?' she asked him angrily in the High Street outside.

He grinned. 'Don't know what you mean, darling.'

'In plain English, you'd have been happy to pick a fight.'

'Nothing to fight about. No one to fight with.'

'Clive, those people really didn't like that status demonstration stuff.'

'Above their heads, honey.'

'They bloody well knew you were taking the piss out of them! It's not like you. You're not even drunk. What shall I do with you?'

'Just love me,' he said. 'Forgive my foolish ways.'

'I suppose I have to.' She took his arm, 'If you feel tired, to hell with the Civic Society Ball. Just go to bed. Promise.'

'I promise.' He stopped at the side street which led to the shopkeepers' car park. 'What will you do tonight?'

'Don't worry about me.'

'You'll be alone.'

'I am most nights. That's how I like it. It's my choice, darling.'

'Yes.' He kissed her. 'I have to go.' He walked away quickly, as he always did when he left her these days. But walk, she thought, as she went towards the car park, wasn't the *mot juste*: he was making a forced march. The enemy had made a surprise breakthrough and had to be cut off.

Strangely enough, what was in Clive's mind as he made his

way to the main car park wasn't very much different from what was in the enemy's mind that day. (Not that he thought of Stephen in such gladiatorial terms.) He saw himself and Ruth together on the same stretch of moorland, where Stephen saw himself and Robin. The picture was there in his mind and it was startlingly vivid. It was irrelevant that he'd just left Ruth, that he saw her almost every day even if only briefly, and that they regularly spent the whole of the evening and sometimes the afternoon together at her flat. It was irrelevant, too, that they'd never been at that particular spot together and that there wasn't any urgent necessity that they ever should be. He liked the picture – or, rather, it liked him – for more and more frequently it came to him unbidden.

Naturally his and Stephen's positions weren't totally identical. He was, after all, actually an inhabitant of the far country to which Stephen now so often longed to return. And he was about to drive his Mercedes up the steep narrow winding road to Throstlehill to a house within fifteen minutes' walk of the moors. He could see them from his bedroom window. And the view from his bedroom window was in itself simply one of the many delights of living in Throstlehill, one of the many blessings which he never took for granted.

Irrelevant yet again: in Clive's mind and in Stephen's mind was the same picture. And superimposed upon it was another picture, in which the moors rose higher, much higher, and the sky above them seemed somehow more immense. In many respects Clive and Stephen were almost as if of different species. But certain longings they shared with the same intensity.

Four

Anyone in the Charbury district who fancied a flutter on the horses knew Arthur Simmerton's name. He wasn't in the Ladbroke league and didn't want to be, but there's no doubt that he was a millionaire. He didn't look in the least like a bookie. He was tall, thin, neatly but drably dressed, wore rimless spectacles and had large expressionless grey eyes and a small primly pursed mouth. He didn't smoke or drink and didn't like horses or indeed any animal. He had been married for twenty years to a large jolly boozy ex-chorus girl and had no children – which was just as well, because he didn't like children either. His office in a side street off Town Hall Square was large, inhumanly tidy and antiseptic, the furniture and fittings stark and modern and functional. There wasn't a hospitality cabinet and no one who had ever visited him there had ever been offered even a cup of tea: he didn't have to ingratiate himself with anyone. He was always Arthur, never Art or Artie; not, of course, that many people were on Christian name terms with him.

The reason for Donald Lendrick being more than usually nerve-racked on the day of the Parade had been that Arthur Simmerton had phoned him at the mills in the morning. Donald had been inclined to tell his secretary to say he was out: he was due at the Grand in forty-five minutes anyway. But he had sense enough to know that that would be the equivalent of closing his eyes so that Arthur Simmerton would go away. He'd met Arthur Simmerton occasionally at the Charbury Conservative Club and, although he hadn't exchanged more than a few brief words with him, he remembered uncomfortably those large expressionless grey eyes and the small primly pursed mouth. Arthur Simmerton wouldn't go away.

Nevertheless his tone when he spoke to Arthur Simmerton was sharp. 'What the devil do *you* want? And why call me at my office?'

'I'll call you at your home if you prefer it. Can you tell me when you'll be in?' Arthur Simmerton's voice was flat and almost entirely devoid of emotion. Though born and bred in Charbury – his father had been a weaver at, strangely enough, Lendrick Mills for thirty years – he didn't have any trace of a Yorkshire accent. He gave the impression that he'd long since rejected it as superfluous, just as he rejected colour in his clothes and in his office.

'No, ro. Might as well settle the matter now.'

'You're putting the cheque in the post?'

'Naturally. I've been rather busy recently. Run off my feet. You know how it is – ' Donald snickered weakly.

'Run off your feet?' Arthur Simmerton repeated the phrase as if it were startlingly original and, indeed, bizarre. 'It's five weeks. You've had four notifications.'

'The matter's in hand.' He started to become genuinely angry. 'Good God, man, you know me! You know what my standing is. I'm not going to run away.'

'You owe me five thousand pounds. Please put the cheque in the post today.'

'You'll be paid. Although I don't have to. But it's a debt of honour . . . ' Donald's voice trailed away.

'A debt of honour?' There wasn't even a hint of a sneer in Arthur Simmerton's voice, but again it was as if it were the first time he'd heard the phrase. 'You owe me five thousand pounds, Mr Lendrick. Pay me immediately.' He hung up.

Donald put the phone down, pain gnawing his stomach. It was the worst yet; and his head was aching too. *I'm not going to run away*: there's nothing I'd like better, he thought bitterly. Would Clive ever be talked to like that by a creature like Arthur Simmerton? No, he wouldn't. He didn't owe money to anyone, much less a bookie, and when he'd fallen ill he'd been stricken suddenly and dramatically and had made a textbook recovery. Clive had respect, Clive had sympathy: a massive heart attack is like a war wound, even has a certain glamour, but nervous dyspepsia is faintly comic, it's somehow felt to be the sufferer's own fault. And he daren't take any more antacid tablets because he'd already exceeded his ration and there'd be the risk of diarrhoea.

He did honestly love Clive. He'd always had a sort of hero-worship for him. They were a good team, they were Jack Sprat and his wife. Lendrick and Sons had survived and flourished because, at the cost of nervous dyspepsia and half a dozen ailments besides, he could always do the essential chores Clive couldn't be bothered with; and Clive at the awful moment when the audience was beginning to yawn and shuffle its feet and cough continually and rustle its programmes would stroll onstage smiling, really taking his time, his hands in his pockets, not giving a damn. He, Donald, always did give a damn. But Clive just stood there, so to speak, in faultless evening dress and belted out loud and clear the very songs the audience wanted. And everyone would be on their feet in the end clapping and cheering, and if they were throwing anything it would be bank notes and flowers and invitations to a champagne supper. But who did the donkey work, who kept the wheels turning, who was the other son in Lendrick and Sons?

Donald didn't put together his feelings quite so resentfully or dashingly. But as he picked up the phone to order a pot of tea from his secretary, he emphatically didn't love Clive in the least. And he was depressed by his rather drab office, unfavourably comparing it with Clive's larger, brighter and more luxurious one. Donald's office was drab and sparsely furnished entirely from his own choice. He really wished to appear badly done by, and indeed Clive had once said as much to him. He didn't, however, remember this, but stared gloomily at the warm black and red carpet, dark green steel filing cabinets and large framed black and white photos of the mills, the weaving shed and the last royal visit, as if about to complain loudly and tearfully that anything was good enough for poor old Donald. In roughly equal proportions, self-pity, resentment, bellyache and fear assailed him. The tea would help when it came: but if he had too much of it he'd want to pee all the time. He rubbed his chest over the heart as the pain increased, trying not to remember Arthur Simmerton's voice.

He wasn't aware that just at the moment his secretary brought him in his tea, Arthur Simmerton was phoning Bruce Kelvedon at his flat in Harrogate. The flat, a large modern one with a view of the Stray, was furnished with a sort of neutral opulence; Bruce in his rather too Thirties blue polka-dot silk dressing-gown looked as if he had every right to be there but was just passing through. His real home was now in New York City. The conversation which he'd begun with Arthur Simmerton would, he hoped, continue a chain of events which would take him and Tracy even further, make them even freer.

'I did what you suggested,' Arthur Simmerton said.

'You would have done anyway.' Bruce took a cup of coffee from Tracy and smiled at her. 'Push him hard now.'

'I can't imagine why he doesn't go to the obvious place for assistance.'

'He won't. I'm not going to explain why.'

'It's of no importance that you should. But I myself could go to that quarter.'

Bruce frowned. 'I shouldn't like that though. And though I'm not an expert in these matters, I don't think that it would be good for you professionally.' His tone was very mild, but he gripped the phone so tightly that his knuckles whitened.

'That argument has some force. But you did offer me inducements.'

Bruce relaxed his grip on the phone. 'The inducements remain.'

46

'Very well. I'll be in touch.' Arthur Simmerton hung up.

Bruce put the phone down slowly. 'I always thought I was pretty ruthless, but Simmerton gives me the creeps.'

'You're not the tiniest bit ruthless. But what I know of that character I don't like.'

'You have to use the material closest to hand. But Simmerton – Christ, I'd really hate to owe him money!'

'That's not ever going to be your problem, honey. But let's you and I keep our noses clean and our big mouths shut.'

'Even when we're alone?'

Tracy lit a cigarette. 'Most of all then. Business is a game, honey. It isn't why we're here. It doesn't matter very much where *here* is. You reading me?'

Bruce's face was blank for a second, then cleared. 'Very clearly. And I like it.'

She sat on the arm of his chair. 'I'll help you get what you want, baby. But you remember this good: I'm always part of the deal. And don't ride anyone too damned hard.'

'I'll remember,' he said. 'As if I'd forget . . . ' And he went on to speak with unreserved sincerity about love; listening with pleasure she failed to see that he was making reservations in other directions.

Some eight hours later Robin was discussing loose covers and curtains with her daughter Petronella and beginning to be aware that Petronella's eyes were sliding away from the pattern books and she wasn't even going through the motions of listening. They were sitting in what had once been called the drawing-room but now, possibly because of the large leather-topped desk and fitted bookcase taking up the whole of one wall, was called the study. It was the largest room in a house of large rooms, easily accommodating in addition to the desk and bookcase, a three-piece suite (the sofa was, of course, a three-seater), two large Parker-Knoll fireside chairs, a three-seater buttoned leather sofa, a TV, a hi-fi unit, a magazine rack, three coffee tables, and a long drinks table.

Whatever size was the right size, this room was the right size, particularly as far as Clive was concerned. Robin mostly preferred to use the morning-room and the kitchen and, increasingly, her own bedroom (which once had been hers and Clive's). She didn't object to the study, but rarely occupied it by herself.

'I'd have welcomed your opinion,' she said to Petronella, pushing the pattern books aside. 'You have a good eye.'

'You'll choose what you like,' Petronella said sulkily.

Robin reflected that Petronella's brand of good looks – dark hair, dark brown eyes, long and somehow coltish legs – didn't go well with sulkiness. She tried to put it into words. 'You should be like the sundial and tell only the happy hours.'

'I don't know what you mean.' Petronella now looked suspicious. That didn't suit her either.

'Don't act dumb. And don't be so ungracious. Can't you see that I *don't* want the same again? You might have had some new ideas.'

'You wouldn't like them.' Petronella fished a packet of cigarettes from the pocket of her jeans and lit her cigarette with a silver Dunhill lighter which once had been Clive's.

'Don't be so sure.'

'I don't inhabit the world of new loose covers and new curtains, Mummy. What's wrong with the old ones?'

'They're rather shabby. I'd like something brighter, anyway.'

'No you wouldn't. You'd like something just like before. In pastel shades which'll stand up to cleaning.' Petronella drifted over to the drinks table. 'Mind if I have a Campari?'

'Not as long as it's a small one.'

'Booze isn't my thing.' Petronella put ice on top of half an inch of Campari and squirted in soda; the red liquid turned pink. 'Do you want one?'

'Give me a Scotch on the rocks. Not too much. No, a little more. Fine.' She took the drink from Petronella and it was even better than she had anticipated, vividly warming yet refreshingly cold, fiery yet bland, a smooth-talking handsome salesman with a big well-shod foot in the door. If only she concentrated on his patter, she wouldn't hear Stephen Belgard's harsh voice. She took another sip of the Scotch and thought of her new dress for the Civic Society Ball – chiffon, near gold, festively daring and highly romantic – and the music would be as she preferred it, strict tempo, loud and clear, but with a touch of melancholy. There wouldn't be any rapture around at the Civic Society Ball, but at least she wouldn't be walking on knives.

Petronella had now flopped down on the leather sofa, putting her drink on the table beside it. The drink, as always, was on the extreme edge of the table. The ash on her cigarette was lengthening and nowhere near the ashtray. Robin frowned at her; she looked sulky, then shook the ash off her cigarette into the ashtray and moved the glass. 'Mummy, have you ever thought of taking a job?'

'I have a job, darling.' Robin was touched by the eagerness which suddenly illuminated Petronella's face. Her voice was now younger and fresher and there was even love there.

'That's just a tax fiddle. Doesn't mean a damned thing. I mean a real job. Something which would – well, *stretch* you . . .'

'Sounds uncomfortable.' She paused: Petronella looked hurt. 'Darling, I didn't mean that – I do see what you mean. But a job that stretches you – you've got to want to do it. You have to *want* something – ' She paused, and took another drink. 'It's got to be – *outside*.'

'You don't really want to go very far away, do you?' Petronella asked.

'Not very far,' Robin said. She noticed that her Scotch was nearly finished and found herself walking over to the drinks table to freshen it up.

'It's time you did go outside,' Petronella said in a low voice, as if afraid of starting some kind of avalanche.

'I might consider it,' Robin said, going back to the sofa. It was a strange conversation, she thought, and a strange light –

as if the sun was reluctant to go down, refusing to let in the darkness. She heard the sound of a car engine outside. 'That's your father.' She looked at her watch. 'My God! I'd better get ready.'

'There's no rush,' Petronella said. 'You don't have far to go, do you?' Her voice was flat now.

As Clive got out of his Mercedes he saw the lights come on at the window of the study. This was one of the many things he took pleasure from. And indeed he could hardly remember a time when he hadn't been glad to come home to Tower House: it was rather too square and resolutely plain to be ever considered beautiful and the square tower at the left (with a workroom on the ground floor and a room above crammed with junk) had always seemed to him a rather odd after-thought. So, too, did the glass-sided front porch. But it had been built in the Edwardian era, when not only materials and workmanship but also interior design were first-rate. It was solid and unshakeable and always welcoming and comfort-assuring. It welcomed him now and its biscuit-coloured stone seemed to him to have an almost animal texture and warmth; now at ten to seven the sky was tinged red and pink and a deepening blue and the colour of the stone was no longer exactly biscuit but the colour of a Golden Labrador. It was healthly stone, both enduring and high-spirited.

The sun was still above the horizon and there was no doubt this year about the spring having arrived. Throstlehill was a moorland village, still with its own identity, though it was now safe and cosy with all amenities and main services. But it stood a thousand feet above sea level, and when a light breeze sprang up Clive briefly felt that, although the weather was mild and the evenings drawing out, in the high fells of North Yorkshire there'd still be patches of snow well past Easter. This wasn't really consciously articulated: he caught the scent of coldness and remoteness and was happy, and more than happy.

Tower House stood at the end of Chipfield Close, a short cul-de-sac with only eight other houses on it, all large, all detached, none of them alike. Lights were on in all the houses: this, Clive thought, was the hour when, if Mummy was lucky, Daddy came home after a long hard day at the office. In three instances in Chipfield Close Mummy had a long hard day at the office too. Clive stood for a moment, still not unhappy. It was very quiet. Clive liked this hour of the day, he liked the feeling of somehow being caught up in a normal and sane but not dull routine. The satisfaction he got from this moment of coming home was like listening to a bugle call by a bugler who really knew his business – yes, it was merely a convenient way of announcing a meal or lights out or whatever it might be, but for a second your soul would leave your body.

And then without any sort of warning he was disorientated: he didn't hear the bugle. He wasn't glad to be returning home. But he wasn't frightened either.

It's important to remember this about Clive. He wasn't in the usual sense of the term old-fashioned, he never tried hard to be a pukka sahib. He didn't place great store upon having been at a public school. He could never quite understand the old school tie mystique. And whilst he never could be bothered to poke fun at it, nevertheless it always struck him as being rather comic. He really wasn't bothered whether he was a gentleman or not.

He wanted his life to flow, without having to sweat unduly about organizing it. He didn't want it to be so inflexibly full that there wouldn't be space for serendipities. Nevertheless he lived by the rules. Occasionally he asked himself awkward questions. Sometimes he longed fiercely to get beyond the boundaries of the commonplace. But that evening he hadn't heard the bugle.

And as he went into the study he knew why he hadn't heard it. There hadn't, he was sure, been a quarrel; but there was an atmosphere of confidences. Both mother and daughter gave him – or rather issued him, like stamps at the Post Office, with quick smiles. He gave them each a quick kiss. Phrases were exchanged not much different in kind from the phrases exchanged with the guests at the Lendrick Parade. He poured himself a small Scotch and topped it up with soda, noticing with some surprise that Robin was making short work of her own drink. He put his glass down untasted.

'I've had enough if I'm going to drive,' he said. 'I don't want a session with the breathalyser . . . I'd better change.'

'I won't be a moment,' Robin said.

'There's no rush. They won't mind starting without us.' Suddenly he remembered a line from a song, remembered the song not the singer: *And life goes on without me . . .*

'No, they won't mind, Daddy,' Petronella said angrily. 'And you don't really want to go, anyway.'

'Don't get so fraught about it, love,' Clive said mildly. The song sidled into his head again: *Just a gigolo, everybody knows, Everybody knows the part I'm playing . . .*

'You could have come,' Robin said sharply to Petronella.

'Not my scene. Anyway, Olive and Vanessa are dropping in later.'

'Good,' Clive said. 'This house is too damned big for you to be alone in. Bloody ridiculous, really. Time we looked for something smaller.' *When the end comes I know They'll say just another gigolo . . .* The song wouldn't leave him alone, it was wearing him down.

'This house suits me,' Robin said fiercely. 'It always has suited me. And I'm going to get new loose covers. And new curtains. Yes, and new carpet. This is my home –' Clive felt surprise again: she didn't generally speak so quickly or so loudly.

'Why all the emotion?' He remembered what Ruth had told him, then decided to forget it; least said, soonest mended. 'It was just idle curiosity. Do what you want, love.'

'It's not a question of what I want. It's a question of what the house wants.'

'That's a very pretty thought.' Suddenly the song had left him, but the pressure hadn't lifted.

52

'Yes, isn't it?' She looked at him searchingly. 'But don't pretend that it isn't clear to you.'

'I'd just as soon not go into it,' he said. 'What's the point?' He saw with some concern that Petronella was looking a little puzzled, even a little frightened. He smiled at her reassuringly. 'All right, Petronella, I won't make waves.'

He rose suddenly and walked quickly out of the room. If Ruth had been there, she would again have noted that his pace was the pace of a forced march. He slowed down going up the broad staircase, gripping the polished oak bannisters, making himself take it easy, but not too easy. Through the window, at the turn of the stairs, he could see that it still wasn't twilight and found himself impatient for the darkness and, perversely, wanting coldness too, darkness and coldness and the evenings drawing in instead of the evenings drawing out.

Five

Oddly enough, soon after Clive's arrival at Tower House a cool breeze sprang up in the Wey Valley, died away for a while, then returned in greater strength, carrying light showers with it, becoming still cooler. The showers became heavy and at eleven o'clock, as Jean and Stephen sat in their drawing-room, there was a feeling in the air of late winter rather than of early spring. Stephen sensed it and didn't mind; Jean sensed it and resented it.

The drawing-room was as large as the study at Tower House and didn't contain much more furniture. Nevertheless, it looked more crowded, was even rather claustrophobic: the new red flock wallpaper (almost exactly the same shade as in the studio at their previous house in Kensington) and the very fussy wall lights with blue velvet tasselled shades contributed to this. But it was a warm room, a comfortable room, a room in which there would never be any worries about money.

This was in fact – though they didn't talk about it very much – a great bond between Stephen and Jean. It wasn't that they liked money in the sense that it was the most important thing in their lives. It was that money liked them. Neither of them would ever be rich rich, super-rich: they both put other things first. But neither would ever be poor, no matter what disasters assailed them.

Each of them was *there* professionally in a place from which they couldn't be dislodged by anything much short of sudden death. Either of them was free to walk out on the other and they wouldn't have to count up their money to see if they could afford the petrol or the train fare or a hotel room. Even in supposedly well-heeled Weybridge, surprisingly few were in their position. Husbands as well as wives would go home to Mother, there being nowhere else where they could go.

So the silence between them wasn't hostile. They weren't chained together, they weren't prisoners. Stephen could, after all, afford to rent a cottage in Hailton merely on impulse, and had already worked out a way of making it tax-deductible. He was actually still not wholly serious about the idea, still hadn't committed himself. It wasn't so long since he'd gone into the nursery to peep at his sleeping son – outside the rumpled bedclothes as usual, arms and legs spread out, his small rosy face scowling as if he'd been fighting sleep to the very end. Thinking about his son, he put Robin firmly out of his mind.

'Christ, I'm tired!' he said. 'I thought those silly buggers would never go.'

'It's not eleven yet,' she said mildly. 'They weren't all that bad.'

'Could've been worse. The women rabbited on rather.'

She smiled. 'All right, love. But they're our neighbours. We might as well be on good terms with them.'

'Beverley went on about that too. All about the wonderful togetherness in the shitty mining village where her old Dad was the Beloved Physician. The bloody working classes never let anyone but relations pass their threshold. They keep themselves to themselves. Not that they like their relations very much.'

'You really have suffered, darling.' She yawned. 'Did I tell you Marcus phoned yesterday?'

'You didn't, actually.' He frowned. 'Were you frightened to?'

'Why should I be? It was very casual. Bags of what he imagines to be old-world charm. He's actually finding out when I'll be available. For what I don't know.'

'He's a devious sod! I can ask around.'

'I suppose it wouldn't do any harm. I don't have to commit myself. On the other hand, someone might be on the point of *asking* me . . . It's nice to be asked.'

'I think you're getting restless,' he said. 'Despite your desire to be a dedicated Mum.'

'Restless? Not really. I think you're the one who's restless. It's time you settled down.'

'Settled down? I couldn't be more settled down. Here I am in deepest Surrey, having just entertained our charming neighbours the lawyer and the town planner and their charming wives with their charming fat legs. *Short* fat legs. Tessa's are short enough, God knows, but it's a miracle Beverley's arse doesn't scrape the ground.' He grinned at her. '*Your* legs give the impression of going right up to the shoulders. Ian's eyes were out on stalks.'

She looked down at her black-stockinged legs with complacency. 'He only glanced discreetly when Beverley wasn't looking.' She sighed. 'He's content as he is. I wish you were more like him.'

'Oh, Christ, do I have to smoke a pipe? And use a lot of matches? And puff out a lot of smoke?' He lit another cheroot. 'Mind you, I might manage that. It's the wise mature expression which would be beyond me.'

'I think it would,' she said dispassionately. 'Your most frequent expression is one of derision. You're so sure that you're much much cleverer than anybody else.'

'I don't look at you like that.' His tone was defensive.

'You wouldn't dare. Because I'm not really dependent upon you. I can bugger off any time I want. And take Julian.'

'What the hell are you talking about?'

'You needn't sound so agitated. I'm just pointing out a simple fact. As you do often. Like you did tonight when you said to Roland with a merry laugh that all public buildings since the War were badly designed, totally hideous, and jerrybuilt.'

'That was a joke. Why the hell should you care anyway?'

'I don't care. In my own imperfect way I'm just trying to tell you what I want.'

'What would that be?' His expression was now one of genuine bewilderment.

'Rather more commitment. More reaching out. More real sharing.'

'Oh God, that's bloody jargon! Bloody togetherness again –'

'Don't bloody well try to put me down!' She raised her voice for the first time. 'You know damned well what I want.'

'You've got what you want,' he said. 'I can't give you any more.'

'I think you could. There's a lot more you can give. Once you settle down. You haven't much time.'

'Giving. Settling down. Togetherness. You're talking like that bloody Beverley again.'

'Beverley knows where she is. So does Tessa.'

'Tessa? Oh, yes. Not so much to say for herself. Reserved, that's what Tessa is.' His voice was now querulous, almost whining. 'I wish I knew what the hell you were going on about.'

Jean rose in one graceful movement. 'You're not *absolutely* sure that you're cleverer than me, are you?' She drifted to the door, then turned. 'Tell you what, though. I'm a better fuck than Beverley or Tessa. Or any other woman. *Anywhere.*'

Her last words to Stephen as she left the room were of no importance, though once again that day she'd made a first-class professional exit, enjoyed by them both. But she had really been delivering serious warnings which were as much for his benefit as hers. If the quality of his commonsense (which is to say his sense of self-preservation) had been equal to the quality of his intellect he would have listened to her more attentively.

But the lives of even men as intelligent as Stephen bear a curious resemblance to the opening chapter in the traditional horror story. The rubicund village innkeeper blanches when the Old Manor is mentioned. Things have happened there which don't bear talking about. They say – and then he lowers his voice to talk about the things which don't bear talking about. And no one has seen the face of the new Squire, but he bain't like the old 'un, that he bain't. And the carriage hired at double fare turns at the entrance to the drive, dashing away, the hero can't help thinking, as if the hounds of hell were after it. And as he trudges up the long winding drive, a piercingly cold wind springs up, owls hoot, bats squeak, and anguished screams and unearthly music are heard. Black-hooded riders on black foaming-mouthed horses gallop by, following a pack of ravening black mastiffs. The hero plods on towards the black lowering bulk of the Old Manor, not even disturbed by the fact that the light blazing from its huge windows, instead of the usual cheerful orange, is a sepulchral blue.

Roughly this is how it was with Stephen. He had an impossible dream and, being one of a small privileged minority, was confident that he had the means to realize it. (Being morally rather confused, he was also confident that he was entitled to.) He was, though he wasn't aware of it, a romantic, like many men of his generation, like Clive and Robin, in fact, though they were romantics of a different kind. Stephen would have strenuously denied this: he saw himself as being exceptionally and unremittingly clear-sighted and rational, free of all the bourgeois illusions and free of all the proletarian illusions too, but generous and fair on top of it. He always loudly and resoundingly proclaimed himself to have no other motive except self-interest, but secretly he cherished the notion that all those fortunate enough to work with him would refer to him as Stephen the Just. Somehow he was a hero and what he wanted was right.

This was mostly a consequence of history, of his having been a soldier in absolutely the last was with foreseeable and acceptable limits. He hadn't been a soldier for very long and had, quite understandably, been glad to have been invalided out of the Army after Dunkirk, but the War had shaped him, would always be with him, just as Clive's shrapnel scar would always be with him.

Things were different with Norman Radstock and his friend Gary. They were of later generations: they knew that the lights would go up and they'd go out into the cold and the dark and as likely as not be knocked down by a bus. They both lived almost exclusively in the measurable and tangible present. They weren't romantics at all, though they both often said they were. What this meant, however, was that they were both fond of, for example, Asti Spumante, bright silks, chocolate liqueurs, spectacular sunsets and songs like 'I'll See You Again' and 'Deep in My Heart'. Norman had done his National Service in the Army in the Fifties all in England and mostly in Catterick counting stores: it hadn't been an oppressively unpleasant period in his life but he never now felt it worth remembering. Gary, ten years younger than him, had escaped it.

Even if he'd been Norman's age, he would have somehow escaped it, and not by shaving his armpits and painting his fingernails red either, much less chewing cordite. He'd have found another way. Gary was that sort of person. People said that he always fell on his feet; and there's no denying that he was rather like a cat in this respect. But he didn't need nine lives: he always managed to be in a position where he didn't have to lose even one.

He had come to Hailton from Leeds late in 1967 following the death of his father and mother in their 1960 Vauxhall Cresta on the A1 just past Durham. His father, with efficiency but no enthusiasm, had been manager of a small hardware shop, his mother a hairdresser. Next to their 1930 pebble-dashed semi-detached house on the road to Headingley they had loved the Cresta. It was a typical British car of the Sixties, with duo-tone paintwork, a lot of chrome and curves which were both bloated and constricted. It tried hard to look like a Cadillac, or a Lincoln, or a huge and arrogant distance-devourer, fit for a president, a gangster or a film star, and it gave Gary's parents many hours of pure happiness until it killed them.

But this isn't fair to the Cresta. Gary's father had taken a nightschool course in car maintenance and, a week before the crash, had been tinkering with the steering assembly. Getting it spot-on, he said to his next-door neighbour. 'Five minutes' work. The bloody garage'd charge you twenty quid for that.' So the Cresta had gone under an articulated lorry at sixty and had burst into flames. It took Gary's parents, trapped under the lorry, a full thirteen minutes to die.

Gary sold the house – the mortgage was paid off – and cashed in the insurance policies. What his father had often said was absolutely true: he was worth more dead than alive. His mother had squirrelled away a sizeable amount too. His father's imperfect understanding of the Cresta's steering assembly hadn't made him rich, but he had enough to give up his job in the furniture shop in Leeds where he'd begun to realize he was getting nowhere very fast and buy Elaine's Gift Shop in Hailton. The small flat above the shop was exactly what he'd always wanted: a decent-sized lounge, a bedroom with built-in wardrobes and large enough to accommodate a double bed comfortably, a small kitchen which was a kitchen and not a kitchenette, and a newly decorated bathroom with a brand-new shower, bath, WC, washbowl and bidet. Shocking pink wouldn't have been his choice for the wall tiles or emerald green for the fittings, or chrome yellow for the floor, but it was uproariously cheerful. His parents' house, although in good order and regularly redecorated, had always been drab and depressing. Whatever hankering after colour and luxury his parents had had been expended on the Cresta, which had every accessory and fitting a car could have, including fake leopardskin seat-covers.

Gary was, of course, damaged. His parents had never ill-treated him or in the strict legal sense neglected him, but they hadn't ever wanted any children and took good care not to have any more. They were really completely fulfilled having each other, and the house and the Cresta: he'd always felt that he was an intruder. The flat above the shop was his, just as the shop was, and his Morris Minor 1000 Traveller was simply transportation and had no extras except a radio.

Norman had left Gary's bed a little after Stephen had got into bed with Jean some two hundred miles away, and had discovered, agreeably surprised, that their quickie in the afternoon and rather too many Martinis and too much avocado with prawns, coq au vin and green salad and Mateus Rosé and meringue glacé and Armagnac and being rather under stress didn't prevent him from being fully as vigorous as in his twenties. But throughout the act, with his eyes open, knowing where he was and who he was with, he'd had another place and another person on his mind. He dreamed an impossible dream.

Norman was in Gary's flat and nowhere else and with Gary and with no one else. Norman knew when he was well off, though he wouldn't have expressed it quite as crassly as that. Certainly at the moment he emerged from the bathroom smelling of Eau Sauvage he had no dreams of being anywhere else but where he was, or with any other person but Gary. It was irrelevant that he was going home soon to the flat he shared with Ruth in Charbury. Gary was his love, Gary had unfrozen him, Gary had released him.

For Norman had been damaged much more severely than Gary: his mother, his father, his two boisterously masculine brothers had wanted him too much, had expected too much of him, and their clumsy kindness had been hardest of all to bear. He'd drifted from his National Service to Charbury University and a mediocre history degree, and from there into bookselling in Birmingham and London, and had met Ruth at a booksellers' conference in London not long before the opportunity to buy the bookshop in Hailton had come up. His friendship with Ruth had been immediate – asexual and undemanding, but always sustaining. His father, the head of an old-established firm of Doncaster accountants, had lent him the money he needed without question. Ruth had had a substantial legacy and the bookshop too had been a success from the first. And his design for living had been, though not exactly admirable, perfect for him: as he'd said to Robin, he'd hidden in the long grass from the nasty men with guns.

He'd been quite smug and cosy, the design for living had taken in Clive, which meant Clive and Ruth, and no one ever expected from him any more than he could give. He had never had any sex life at all in the usual sense, though in another sense since coming to Hailton he'd always felt completely fulfilled. As he used to put it frequently, in order to enjoy a flower, you don't have to pluck it. And then last spring quite without reason he knew that he had to go, to make a dash for it out of the long grass. And the chance had come up of the partnership in a thriving bookshop in Surrey and negotiations had begun. He wasn't dissatisfied with Hailton, he wasn't lured by the South. He had to go and that was all there was to it. Then in the summer he'd met Gary and now he still was very much in Yorkshire, happy as never before, dressing with an actor's between-scenes quickness beside the double bed where Gary lay naked and complacently shameless on top of the rumpled pink sheets and black satin coverlet with a pattern of red dragons.

'You're in a great hurry to be off,' Gary said. He was small – perhaps half an inch taller than Norman – but stockier, with wide shoulders and a deep chest. His voice was pleasantly resonant, at times a boom, somehow old-fashioned in quality. His accent wasn't quite as camp as Norman's, but like Norman's it was classless, not true Received English, but near enough to make no difference, since actually to be received at Court wasn't one of his ambitions.

'I've a lot of chores to do tomorrow,' Norman said. This wasn't true; and not to go home to Charbury would have given him more time to do the chores if it had been. But he didn't feel equal to explaining that Ruth would actually be waiting up for him, that he needed a nightcap and a chat with her, that he needed also to sleep alone in his own room, needed to sleep alone in order that he might then be more at one with Gary, that he'd be able to love him without the distraction of his physical presence. He could simply phone

Ruth if he wanted to stay with Gary and naturally she wouldn't object; but it wouldn't be according to their design for living. He smiled at Gary. 'I really do hate to leave you.'

'You always do just the same.' Gary didn't really seem angry. He got up and took a red silk dressing-gown out of the wardrobe. 'Fancy a cuppa?'

'That would be lovely.'

'You can have anything you like, dear.' He deftly buttoned Norman's shirt for him, then took up his white silk tie with the pattern of pink hearts. 'I do fancy this.'

'It's yours,' said Norman.

'Thank you very much,' Gary said. He whisked it into the wardrobe, then opened the wardrobe door again. 'No, I was only joking.'

'I don't care. I want you to have it. As long as it gives you pleasure . . .'

Gary's round rosy face became radiant: it was what Norman termed in his more sardonic moods his Sir Galahad and the Holy Grail expression. The thick curly chestnut hair helped too. 'It's just what I want for that cashmere jacket.'

'Not with cashmere – ' Norman began, then stopped. 'Please yourself, honey. You're young. You can get away with anything.'

'You're not so old,' Gary said. 'You certainly don't act it.' He glanced at the bed. The words and the enunciation, the coy glance and the choirboy face and his resonant baritone produced an odd dissonance. For a split second Norman wasn't sure that he liked it, then he decided to accept it as a borderline *frisson*. Gary, after all, gave him more pleasure than pain. He refused to believe that he was a gold-digger, he was in fact touchingly insistent on paying his way – they stood each other dinner or the theatre or a concert, or whatever it might be in turn, as friends do – as for that matter he and Ruth did. And what the hell did a tie matter?

'Don't think I'm not grateful,' Norman said, and patted Gary's cheek. It was very soft with a feminine smoothness though Gary was in the essential respects superabundantly and even frighteningly masculine.

'That goes both ways,' Gary said. He went into the kitchen, followed by Norman. He filled the kettle, plugged it in, set out on the small pale-blue Formica-topped table two glasses in metal Russian glass-holders, sliced a lemon into wafer-thin slices, put the slices into a small amber-coloured glass bowl, put the bowl on the table, each movement deft and quick. 'You shouldn't go on so much about your age, Norman. It gets on my nerves, it really does. You're not forty yet, for heaven's sake . . . '

'Not so damned far off. And things are getting tougher.'

Gary sat down, picked up a packet of Balkan Sobranie Cocktail cigarettes, took out a pink and a mauve cigarette, lit them both with a solid silver initialled Dunhill lighter – a present from Norman – and handed Norman the mauve one. This, like the lemon tea in glasses without sugar, was one of the bonds between them. They smoked only after sundown and never in the bedroom. They smoked cigarettes with a tinge of the exotic, like Gauloise, Sullivan, Camel, Black Sobranie and the Sobranie Cocktail themselves, and never inhaled. Both had tried cannabis, but were too cautious to make a habit of it.

'Tougher? In the book trade?' Gary laughed showing dazzlingly perfect white teeth. They were more cap than dentine, the work of the most expensive dentist in Leeds, and they were yet another agreeable consequence of his father's mistaken half-turns of the spanner on two small nuts in the Cresta steering assembly. This thought didn't occur to him then, but it was always plodding along at a great distance behind him, never losing sight of him. When he was Norman's age, the tortoise would catch up the hare and the hare wouldn't enjoy it. But that was in the future. He got up and made the tea. 'Don't look so hurt, Norman,' he said. 'You jog along very nicely. You know where you are with books. And you've got steady customers like the Training College lot. But gift shops – either you haven't enough of what the buggers want and you lose money, or you've got too much and you lose money. And God only knows what they do want!'

Norman sipped his tea, glad of its soothing warmth. 'Elaine seems to have known what they wanted.'

'So she should have done. She had this shop for nearly forty years. She treasured each customer. I bet she knew each one of them. Elaine's Gift Shop is an institution, a good old Hailton institution.'

'What's wrong with that?'

'Just about all Elaine's customers are geriatric by now. One can't buy bric-à-brac from beyond the Great Divide. There'll have to be a change.'

Now Gary's tone was serious, no longer the usual shop-keeper's mild grumble. 'How much of a change?' Norman asked.

'Radical. And there's got to be restocking. And a huge clearout.' He rapped out the details down to the smallest measurement, particularizing each shade of the new interior decorations, and presenting in a matter of minutes a picture of a new Elaine's, clean and bright but not scrubbed and strident, with more space yet more intimacy, where every article, by reason of its being properly displayed, would give the customer the impression that if they didn't buy it immediately someone else would, it being, because of its supreme desirability, the last one in stock.

'God, it'll cost a fortune!' Norman said.

'You're absolutely right. The more I think of it the more it scares me.' Gary paused, then named a figure.

'My God!' Norman said. 'It'd cost less to redecorate Harrods.' He hesitated. 'But I could help. Half of it anyway –' He was sneering at himself as he was saying it, trying to keep out of his mind the cheap, obvious words *There's no fool like an old fool*, aware that he was making a promise that he'd have to keep. Norman wasn't mean: his affection for Gary was genuine. But it vanished as soon as he uttered the words *half of it*. He still refused to believe that Gary was a gold-digger. He had no option: else where was love? But what couldn't be denied now was that all the ecstasy he'd shared with him since last year had to be paid for at the rate of about fifty pounds per orgasm. He knew that he'd still desire again that smooth strong body and still, having satisfied that desire, have the bonus of an end to any sort of dissatisfaction, still feel not only completely a man but completely feminine too, both taker and taken. And he hated himself for it.

Gary flushed. 'No way! I' wasn't asking you for money. What the hell do you think I am? You're my friend.' His voice softened. 'I've got someone interested. Of course, it's not absolutely nailed on. But I've really gone into it thoroughly with her. She's really serious. Mind you, rich people don't get to be rich by throwing their money about.'

'This is the person you're dining with tomorrow evening?' Norman took another sip of tea and put it down. 'Mind if I have a brandy?'

'Be my guest. Bring the bottle back and I'll have one too.'

Norman in the lounge – once chintzy and now all Habitat furniture, primal colours in a hard-fought contest with large reproductions of Hockney's *Two Boys Bathing*, Bacon's *Screaming Cardinal* and Klee's *Magic Fishes* – stood for a moment with his hand on the brandy bottle fighting back the tears.

Putting two glasses on the table, Gary looked at him with some consternation when he returned. 'Norman, why the hell do you look so upset? Don't stand there. Sit down.'

'I'm all right,' Norman said. He slumped down. 'Why didn't you tell me all this before?'

Gary poured the drinks. 'I told you about the business dinner tomorrow, didn't I?'

'The business dinner. The *business* dinner – ' Norman's voice rose. 'And who with, my darling? Who the bloody hell with?' He was shouting now, his face flushed.

'Take it easy. I've mentioned her before anyway. Miriam

Cothill. Lives near Harrogate.' He looked away from Norman and down at the table.

'How old is she? How old is this business lady?'

Gary sighed. 'Always this age thing. I haven't asked her. I think she's about forty-five. I don't care if she's a hundred and five. To me she's just so much money on the hoof.'

'Forty-five. That's nice. Mother and son.' Norman emptied his glass and poured himself another drink. 'Has she got a husband?'

'She's a rich widow.' Gary glanced at Norman's glass. 'Not that I begrudge it you, but that's a stiff drink.'

Norman didn't seem to have heard. 'You didn't tell me,' he said peevishly. 'You didn't tell me about this woman.'

'Would you have been better pleased if it had been a man?'

Norman took a gulp of brandy. 'Let it go then. It's just that I care about you. Too bloody much. Ridiculous really.' He stood up. 'I'd better be off.'

'I don't think so,' Gary said. 'You really better had stay. Apart from any other consideration, you're not really fit to drive. You're too – emotional. Really and truly tired and emotional.' His voice was gentle.

'I'll cause scandal,' Norman said, trying to smile.

Gary got up and put his arm round Norman's shoulders. 'Silly old thing, who cares these days?'

Norman found the tears coming to his eyes again and this time he couldn't hold them back. He didn't really know why he was weeping. It was a joy and a consolation to lean back and be supported by Gary's firm grip, but he knew he'd pay for it. How he would pay he couldn't surmise, but tears wouldn't be the only coinage demanded. He took out his handkerchief, wiped his eyes and stood up. 'I'll phone Ruth,' he said. 'In case she worries.'

'You do that,' Gary said. 'You'll be all right in the morning, love.'

'Oh, yes,' Norman said. He found his throat was suddenly sore. 'I'm always fine in the morning.' His voice had become a croak.

Six

The morning after the Parade started off for Clive with a cheque from his broker. He passed it to Petronella, grinning. 'Unto him that hath shall be given.'

Petronella glared at the cheque, then at Clive. The morning wasn't her best time. And though the St Perpetua's uniform – mid-blue blazer, dark blue skirt, white shirt and blue and red tie – suited her better than jeans, she always wore it with an air of fierce resentment. 'It's all a racket,' she said, exhaling cigarette smoke noisily. 'Money should be earned by *work*. *Productive* work.'

'Wouldn't be much production, love, if nobody bought shares.' He took back the cheque from Petronella. He didn't expect Robin to be interested: though not an idiot about money and no doubt prepared if needs be to accept the most savage cuts in expenditure unflinchingly, it was nevertheless something on which she'd rarely expended even a moment's thought. She was now absorbed in a letter from her parents in the South of France. He could, of course, show her the cheque when she'd finished the letter, but it wouldn't be any good. Her eyes would rest on the cheque for a split second, and slide away; there'd be a quick smile and a few words and then it would be out of her mind. Two hundred pounds – give or take the shillings and pence – wasn't a fortune, and, after all, he'd done no more than take a tip from a reliable source and sell at the figure he'd set. Still, he would have liked a little praise.

'It's a question of who gets the profit,' Petronella said. 'The money-manipulators or the workers.' She took a gulp of coffee as if forced to drink it at gunpoint: it occurred to him that few young people he met really seemed to enjoy eating and drinking.

'The workers aren't doing so badly,' he said good-humouredly, and took another spoonful of oatmeal. He sometimes longed for bacon and eggs, sausages, fried bread and black pudding, but he'd grown to like the taste of oatmeal: it was filling, it had a comforting innocence, but it wasn't too boringly bland.

'They're not doing so well in textiles,' Petronella said.

'What we produce in Charbury is worsted,' he said. 'High-grade worsted. Super Seventies and upwards. We're still getting by. Absolutely no trouble at t'mill.' He grinned at her, his spirits rising. It was a bright day again, in fact bright in every sense, full of *joie de vivre*. When he'd first opened his eyes there'd been an affability about the sounds from outside; the rattle of empty bottles being carried away by the milkman had seemed positively tuneful and the thud of letters through the letter-box promised only good news. And already he'd registered the fact that, it being warm, cars were starting at the first turn of the ignition key. Not, he reflected, that anyone in Chipfield Close had to leave for work all that early: it wasn't much more than thirteen minutes to Hailton and twenty minutes to Charbury even during what was in this part of England only jestingly described as the rush hour. No one in Chipfield Close rushed, nor did they cram into commuter trains. The bigger cars, the company cars, the husbands' cars would leave first, then afterwards the smaller cars, the second cars, the wives' cars, all off in good time, but no one nervous, no one harried, all attending to things in due course. All was as it should be outside: Chipfield Close and the life that was lived there had always been nearly as important to him as the house itself.

The kitchen was on the right-hand side of the house with a gap between it and the garage. Though the one window was big, the garage cut off much of the light. But somehow it was never depressing, always on good terms with the sun. The new half-tiled yellow walls – yellow with a tinge of orange, a warmer shade than the plain lemon yellow walls before –

70

helped, and so did the new pine kitchen units and the new flower-patterned tiled floor. But it had always been rejoicing, it had never been drab. There was every conceivable kitchen appliance here, including a brand-new dishwasher, but it still looked like a kitchen and not an operating theatre. They'd kept the big old pine table and the large beech rush-bottomed chairs and he'd bought a new beech rocking-chair, which lately he'd grown increasingly fond of.

Clive was, in fact, an exceptionally happy person. He wasn't phlegmatic, and his heart attack and convalescence had given him time to think and had sharpened his instincts. He hadn't told Robin that he knew Stephen was reported to be looking for a cottage in Hailton and he hadn't let his knowledge come between him and his sleep either. But he had caught the scent of danger or even calamity. This he put aside now.

He was grateful for the fine day, the oatmeal, the way the kitchen looked and particularly the way the old scrubbed pine table fitted in with the new pine units, the second cup of strong Assam tea, and for talking with Petronella. (One part of his mind had its own thoughts, the other talked to her.) It didn't in the least upset him that he didn't agree with her views. They'd been arguing without rancour for some three minutes when Robin put down her parents' letter and took up another.

'Believe me, your beloved workers are well contented,' Clive said to Petronella. 'There are no labour problems. Unless you count that strike at Denby's. And God only knows what that's about. They're still making Denby raincoats.'

'Daddy, you do not understand.' Petronella's face was slightly flushed, but it wasn't sulky any more. 'There must be control by the workers – '

Robin looked up from her letter. Her face was not shocked, not in any sense ruffled, but her eyes were cold. Petronella broke off. 'I'll have to dash, Daddy.' She stood up.

'Wait a moment,' Robin said. She continued to read the letter.

'What the hell's all this about?' Clive asked.

'Shut up, Clive!' Robin didn't look at him.

Clive felt his head begin to throb. 'Sod that! Don't bloody well ever tell me to shut up! No one does. What the hell's in that letter?'

'Old Kenton's got it in for me,' Petronella said.

'The letter's from St Perpetua's?' Clive took another gulp of tea but didn't enjoy it.

'You'd better read it for yourself,' Robin said. She passed him the letter.

'Kenton has got it in for me,' Petronella said. 'Her bloody favourites get away with murder – '

'Calm down, love,' Clive said. He took out his reading glasses. Once, not so long ago, he'd only used them occasionally: now he was becoming almost unable to manage without them.

'You see how it is,' Robin said, more to herself than anyone else. 'She was until recently very bright and very responsive. Mrs Kenton had high hopes of her . . . '

'You'd better let me read it for myself.' As he skimmed over the tired bureaucratic phrases – *after careful consideration, acting in the best interests of, knowing as a parent myself what your feelings must be* – he became more and more angry, not at Petronella, not at her headmistress, but at Robin sitting there so impassively. It wasn't fair; but it wasn't fair that the smile, so to speak, had been wiped off his face. He put the letter down. 'Well, as Churchill said, there's every known cliché there except "Prepare to Meet Thy God" and "Please Adjust Your Dress Before Leaving",' he said. 'But what she's really saying is that Petronella's not doing a stroke of work herself and not letting anyone else do a stroke of work either. And doing other things. Which aren't described with any degree of precision but – '

'You do note that she refers to Petronella being deeply disturbed,' Robin said.

'Christ, when I wasn't much older than Petronella I was

deeply disturbed too. All these bloody Krauts kept trying to kill me – ' He stopped himself. 'We'd better see Mrs Kenton and try to sort things out. Seems a great fuss about nothing to me.'

'I don't think that your attitude is very helpful,' Robin said.

'It's the only attitude I've got. Hell, all kids can be a bit unruly.'

'George and Roger weren't unruly. We didn't have any letters of complaint about them.'

Petronella stared at them both. 'You're talking as if I weren't here!'

Clive went over to her. 'Look, we'll manage something, love. We'll see Mrs Kenton, we'll make some sense out of it all . . . '

'But not today, of course,' Robin said. 'Not any time today. Particularly not this evening.' Her tone was acid.

'Don't try that on,' Clive said. 'Never mind what the bloody day is.'

'Oh, I'd never dream of disturbing your routine. It's Wednesday, isn't it? That's much more important than your daughter.'

'All right then, let's have it out now, for Christ's sake! Let's hear Petronella's side of it.' His head began to throb.

'Stop it, Daddy,' Petronella said, and moved away from him. 'I'll talk about it with Mummy. When you've gone.'

He took a deep breath. 'All right. You talk about it with her. But don't think that I don't care. I do care. I care very much.'

'We know that, Daddy, we know that,' Petronella said gently. She was standing by Robin now and he noticed their likeness. He didn't notice it very often because of the contrast between Petronella's brown hair – darker than mouse – and Robin's fair hair. But the shape of the face was the same and the large brown eyes were the same; and he could see that they didn't need him. He picked up his briefcase and walked out without a word. The smile had been wiped off the morning person's face in the morning.

And yet by the time he'd turned left into Hailton High Street for Charbury, cheerfulness was beginning again. He had left home full of resentment at Robin – Robin the treaty-breaker, Robin unexpectedly the jealous suburban shrew. On the one hand he felt that she and Petronella were ganging up against him and yet he couldn't help wanting to shield Petronella from a cruel world: it would begin in a small way, he thought, and then work up. He didn't notice the woods which bordered Throstlehill or the newly finished Californian split-level cedar-and-sandstone house at the end of Boggart Road, nearest the village green; it did actually fit in with the village, whilst the other two of its kind in the next road were still obviously unsuited for anywhere else but California. Normally he would have noticed this, just as he would have noticed the way that the land dropped steeply on the double bend half a mile outside the village, the way that the landscape always offered surprises no matter how often one had seen it. It was the rock which did it: and the stone houses and the stone walls which seemed to grow from the rock. The ground was never flat and never rolling but surged with energy, long created and newly creating, always rising, always free. The views were surprises and they gave pleasure: but they were challenges too. And perhaps until he got into Hailton High Street he was in no mood for challenges.

He did, of course, see what he had to see in order to survive, part of his brain giving all the correct orders to his hands and his feet and the Mercedes obeying the orders instantly. He had, after all, been driving for some thirty years and had been driving over this route for some twenty years. But the real Clive, until he reached Hailton High Street, was suffering, couldn't get the scene at breakfast out of his mind, couldn't help feeling unaccountably guilty. Petronella was in trouble, and it wasn't as if she were little and had fallen down and hurt herself. He couldn't pick her up and kiss her and wipe away her tears, he couldn't clean up and bandage her cuts and grazes. But did she need him?

He was aware too that the accommodation which he, Robin and Ruth had arrived at over a year ago was showing signs of strain. It wasn't a highly moral arrangement but it worked, and there was respect and goodwill and no real crises. Now their *détente* was at risk. The letter from Petronella's headmistress had been a frontier incident.

He felt that he couldn't cope, that disorders and every kind of ruin lay ahead and, worst of all, nothing. There was no taste in life and nothing to be done about it. And the letter from Petronella's headmistress was both a detailed and unanswerable indictment and a savage and exemplary sentence against which there was no appeal. He hadn't felt like this before; though he'd suffered hard and heavy blows he'd always been confident that as soon as he got his breath back he'd be in there fighting again. This time he wasn't even consoling himself with the thought that this afternoon and most of the evening he'd be with Ruth. The virus, one might say, was attacking.

But he had more than his share of phagocytes. They called up reserves and repelled the attack. This was despite himself. He didn't say crisply to himself: *Pull yourself together, man.* Or, with an inane grin: *Cheer up, it may never happen.* He didn't even reflect that what the headmistress's letter boiled down to was simply that Petronella was being rather more troublesome than was acceptable and that whatever teenage hell-raising she was indulging in might easily take her somewhere where there wasn't any kindness, where every sound was discordant, where the only option was being a user or being used. After all, there'd been the violent death at Woodstock and Lucy was in the sky with diamonds. Still, the letter was simply an admonition and a warning.

Before the day ended he would work this out and would indeed consciously pull himself together. But phagocytes aren't under anyone's authority. They either leap to the ramparts and drive off the virus or they stay where they are, scratching themselves and swigging their rum ration. Clive was cheerful again by the time he reached the mill because that was his nature. He couldn't have stayed depressed and defeated, even in the remote event of him having wanted to.

Lendrick Mill stood on rising ground above the Central Park. The district was predominantly respectable working-class, the houses stone terrace houses and owner-occupied. Here doorsteps were still yellow-stoned and pavements scrubbed. High above was the once fashionable suburb of Timley; from the fourth floor of the mill the scowling Gothic bulk of Falcon Court, the home of Clive's father, was just visible on the skyline on a clear day. Falcon Court was now a trade union education and conference centre: Clive had no strong feelings about it, and rarely glanced in its direction, but it was important to him that it was there, that the narrow terraced streets were there, that the mill was there, that everything he saw had been there ever since he could remember.

He had never felt that the mill belonged to him. He belonged to the mill. He wasn't sentimental about it, he didn't personalize it. It was too starkly functional for that, built in 1850 of local sandstone, its colour soft grey once but now sooty black and with absolutely no decoration unless one counted the spikes which topped the huge iron gates at the entrance to the mill yard. There were mills in the West Riding, like Manningham Mills in Bradford and Salts Mills at Saltaire, which tried their best to look like palaces – but Lendrick Mill wasn't an expression of anyone's personality. It was simply a large building on four floors where cloth was manufactured, with the offices on the ground floor on each side of the entrance, the garages and the workshop on the left of the mill yard, the yarn store at the back. The chimney, adjacent to the garage, sent no smoke out now, the machinery being electrically driven.

His father, as a half-timer, had used the mill-hands' entrance to the left in the days when it had been the Penny-Hole, penalties for lateness starting at a penny. But

Clive didn't hanker after the past, though the mill was so much part of it. He lived in the present, he had no illusions; just as his father had realized well in advance that fancy worsteds would take over from blue serge, so had he seen the separates revolution coming and concentrated on the higher grades. And if he ever took the present export market for granted, that would be the end of him; he had to see ahead. Nevertheless for him the past was not another country, and his father had been born here and his father before him, and there wasn't any dichotomy between his work and his personal life, any more than there was between Charbury and the hills and open spaces around it. He wasn't ever nowhere, he wasn't ever anonymous, he wasn't ever a stranger. It may safely be assumed that this helped to stiffen the sinews of his phagocytes and to bring him into his office actually looking forward to the day ahead. He hadn't forgotten the letter from Petronella's headmistress. But by the time he'd arrived he'd put it in its proper perspective.

Donald, who'd arrived some ten minutes before Clive, was sitting at his desk half-heartedly going through his mail. He didn't have stomach-ache, and in fact felt extraordinarily well. He wasn't used to this; he suspected with trepidation that the enemy was merely biding its time. He'd had an unpleasant surprise in the mail too but not in connection with his ten-year-old daughter Chloe or his twelve-year-old son Hugh. Large, bright and even-tempered, they were the least of his worries. He'd put the letter from the bank manager down, his hands beginning to shake.

His wife had looked at him with disconcerting steadiness. 'What's the matter?'

'Just the bank being over-cautious.' He'd tried to assume a righteous anger. 'Damned insulting! It wouldn't have been like that with old Trenton . . . ' He stuffed the letter in his pocket.

Chloe and Hugh hadn't noticed anything. Having wolfed

bacon and eggs, they were eating bread and marmalade rather more slowly. But he'd not been able to bear looking at them. He'd not been able to bear looking at them because he loved them. He'd stood up suddenly, knocking over his teacup. 'I'm going to make an early start.'

'Show me the letter,' his wife had said.

'He's just trying it on. He knows I've got the collateral . . . ' He'd not sounded very convincing: Linda had held out her hand.

'Show me the letter,' she'd said. 'Do you think after fourteen years I can't read you like a book?'

And that had been it. In a way it had been a relief. He'd even told her about what he owed to the bookie: and she'd known without being told that he hadn't only been playing the horses. But she'd put that to rights. She was a solicitor's daughter and was conversant with the Gaming Acts. He was too, but any law seemed unreal, a statement of opinion merely, when one had heard Arthur Simmerton's voice. It wasn't cold or even cruel, but dehumanized.

What she'd said after Chloe and Hugh had gone – bouncingly as always and still apparently not having noticed anything amiss – had brought him back to the normal world. She'd tidied up his finances as briskly and breezily as she'd tidied up her ward at Charbury Infirmary where she'd been a Sister. No, you won't pay that Simmerton creature. Collection? Maybe for the really low, who the police wouldn't listen to anyway. Nonsense. You've been watching too much TV. I'll settle that overdraft. Then the ultimatum. No, you won't borrow from Clive. Not again. If you do –

A male outsider seeing Linda would have seen a middle-aged woman with pink-tinted harlequin spectacles, an unremarkable face rather on the square side, and dullish brown hair drawn too tightly into a bun. She was tall for a woman but she was also dumpy. Her blue and orange-flecked tweed suit, her prim and severe shirt-style cream blouse, her ribbed black stockings and black brogues, were as part of her, like an animal's hide. She wore a made-to-measure corset and rarely wore anything that showed the division between her breasts. The effect was as if she had only one full-width breast, cut off square at the sides. Her legs were simply the means of carrying her from place to place.

Donald, however, had the night before seen her naked – literally with her hair down. He knew that she'd got two breasts, and he didn't expect them to be as firm as a young girl's; he knew that they were flesh and had fed his two children. He was fond of her breasts, he was fond of her stretch marks, he was fond of her spare tyre. He didn't expect her to have the flat belly of a boy and indeed preferred roundness. Above all, he liked her soft smooth white skin. In this respect he was similar to Clive: he wasn't a sun-worshipper himself and didn't find suntans particularly attractive, no matter how evenly golden-brown. There was another part of her that he liked, which needn't be particularized, but which he thought about behind locked doors, so to speak. He didn't do this shamefacedly and he didn't isolate that part of her. She certainly didn't isolate the corresponding part of him, but they had their occasional unabashed and tender jokes about it.

Be all this as it may, what Linda gave him he couldn't live without. He didn't, of course, realize that it cut both ways. Linda could be shrewish, Linda was narrow-minded, Linda cared too much about keeping up with the Joneses. Linda was given to envy, particularly of Robin. But she was a normal healthy woman, and in any case she loved him. Her threat to cut off sex if he borrowed money from Clive again was an empty one. She wouldn't have stayed away from his bed for very long.

None of the words which had followed her *or else* were anything else but vague, but Donald had understood immediately. And he'd caved in immediately. He'd understood why she hadn't wanted him to add further to his obligations to

Clive. It would seat Clive even more firmly in the saddle, would push him still further down.

'I could sell him some of my shares,' he'd said.

'He wouldn't take them from you,' she'd said, now really angry. For she knew why Clive wouldn't: legally there would be nothing to stop him but it wouldn't be honourable. It wouldn't be what their father would have wanted. Clive was Chairman and Managing Director and Clive, though no longer having a majority shareholding, had a far bigger shareholding than Donald. He'd feel that he had enough already, that he'd be taking the poor man's one ewe lamb.

Reluctantly she'd respected him for it: but she'd hated him for being the sort of person he was, for being likely to behave far better than she would in his shoes. Donald grimaced. 'Bastard!' he said to himself. 'Smug superior bastard!' Then he shook himself like a dog emerging from water and bent over his mail. This was something he always enjoyed: he was a worrier and a fusspot and not one to make friends and influence people, but he was a born administrator; paperwork was for him a joy rather than a chore.

The phone rang.

'Mr Simmerton,' his secretary said. 'He says it's urgent.'

'Put him through,' Donald said.

'I haven't received your cheque, Mr Lendrick,' Arthur Simmerton said.

'I told you the matter is being dealt with.'

'That means that the cheque hasn't been sent.'

'May I remind you that it's a gaming debt under the definition of the Acts – '

Arthur Simmerton had hung up.

Donald put the phone down slowly. Unlike Clive he'd had no experience of frontline service, having through the freakishness of war served all his time in the Pay Corps in the United Kindom. He'd ended up a Lieutenant and had been at least a square peg in a square hole, though he'd never been enamoured of the Army's system of keeping accounts. Purely by chance, he'd led a very sheltered life. But now he would have almost preferred it if Arthur Simmerton had been a real heavy, had said very softly, almost with regret: *You have made a most appalling mistake, Mr Lendrick*. Or even: *It's no fun living in a wheelchair, Mr Lendrick*. Or: *I have a lot of friends, Mr Lendrick: I think you should get to know them*.

He dismissed it from his mind and got to work on his mail again. But it was as if Arthur Simmerton's toneless voice were somehow lingering in the room and menace were all round him like a grey dust which couldn't be blown away. And Arthur Simmerton's silence was there too.

He was glad when Clive came in and put a sheaf of typescript on his desk.

'Frankly, I'm not impressed,' Clive said. 'Though I'm aware that I'm meant to be.'

Donald glanced at the typescript. 'Oh yes. The computer report.'

'Report?' Clive laughed. 'It's a positive work of art. Reads more like a novel. We're managing very well as we are.'

'We've got to keep down the overheads.'

'I rather relish the idea of programming the computer to use up odds and ends of yarn. But would anybody buy the cloth it designed?'

'The computer wouldn't design it. It couldn't. Charley would do the programming.'

'And no doubt he'll enjoy himself. But is it worth the trouble?' He looked very healthy and cheerful, sitting on the edge of the desk in a new fawn suit with a faint plum and green overcheck, a red and green woollen shirt, a plum-coloured woollen tie and gleaming brogues of almost the same shade, with a green silk handkerchief in his breast pocket splayed out with exactly the correct carelessness.

'Putting that aside, the report does propose some very substantial economies. Bruce put a lot of thought into it.'

'I bet he did. I don't trust that bugger.'

'I think you misjudge him. Honestly, Clive, we really must

cut down the overheads.'

'So you keep saying. We won't cut them by spending a fortune.' He laughed. 'You remember what old Councillor Cross used to say. *The best way to save money, lad, is not to spend it.*'

'Councillor Cross has been dead a long time now. You don't change only when you're forced to. You act in good time.' Despite Linda's *or else* he found himself almost tempted to ask Clive for the money he needed to pay off Arthur Simmerton. Yes, Clive was the normal world. And he wouldn't refuse him the money, he wouldn't give him a lecture on the evils of gambling either. And he'd absolutely not tell Linda or anyone else. And the grey dust and the silence would stay away for good.

'I know what the rates stood at when Councillor Cross was Chairman of the Finance Committee,' Clive said. 'And I know what they stand at now. He must have done something right.' He stood up. 'Anyway, I've made a few notes. Concise, witty and devastating. I've got to be off now. I'm seeing Charley at Axesmith's. He has a few ideas to liven up their range.' He paused. 'Oh, I knew I had something to tell you. You remember those software shares we were talking about?'

Donald nodded. He remembered them and Clive had passed on the tip, but he hadn't dared to risk any money.

'Well,' Clive said, 'I got a cheque for two hundred pounds this morning. Old Bumface my broker was surprised when I sold because they were still rising. But you know my policy.' He grinned, innocently pleased. 'They're going down now. Fast.'

Donald achieved a faint smile. 'That's how it goes. Are you coming back this afternoon?'

'Hardly worth it.'

'There's the Federation meeting tonight. I think it's important.'

'We're in agreement about the agenda tonight, aren't we? You don't need me. Seth and his mates have everything fixed up beforehand anyway.' He grinned. 'In a smoke-filled room at the Conservative Club. He's a Machiavellian old bugger . . .'

'You still ought to turn up.' Donald's voice took on a peevish tone. 'And there *are* a few matters which require your attention this afternoon.'

'Nothing that won't wait.' Clive glanced through the window at the bright sky and scudding clouds, then back to Donald. 'You worry too much. Hell, there's plenty to be cheerful about. Count your blessings. Be good, lad.'

He strode out jauntily, unaware of the irritation that he had aroused. Donald sat quite still for a moment after he'd gone, then phoned his secretary for a pot of tea and continued to plough his way through the mail. It couldn't be said that he hated Clive. But he couldn't help envying him his windfall on the software shares, and briefly and bitterly was forced to admit that even if he'd had the spare cash to buy any he would have hung on as long as they were rising and would have lost his shirt in the end. That this would have been his misjudgement rather than his bad luck never occurred to him.

Seven

Half an hour after Clive had left Lendrick Mills, Stephen Belgard sat in his new and spacious but somehow makeshift office at the Saxon TV studios in Essex, listening with no great show of enthusiasm to his friend Graham Sidlow, his fingers drumming on his desk, his eyes directed to the window on his right rather than to Graham. What he saw was a plain so flat as to give the impression of having been artificially levelled, with a scattering of fields and hedges, a new housing estate, two new factories and a ruler-straight new dual carriageway running through it. The predominating materials were red brick and concrete and there seemed to be more cars around than there were human beings. It was a landscape that no one had ever loved or remembered with tears in exile, a landscape not so much morose as apathetic, as indifferent to good weather as to bad, showing not the least gratitude now for the bright spring sunshine and not at all exhilarated by the lively spring breeze.

'It genuinely is a viable proposition,' Graham Sullow said sharply.

Stephen jerked his gaze away from the window. 'Viable? You mean practicable and profitable.' He smiled to remove any sting from the implied slight reproof. He considered Graham to be his friend because they'd worked together once at the BBC and because so far Graham had never tried to do him down. Graham, a large fizzy man with rather chilly and watchful eyes, felt roughly the same towards Stephen.

'I know what it means when you start being pedantic,' Graham said. 'You're not really sold on the idea, are you?'

'Needs a bit of mulling over. So far the vibes aren't good . . .'

The phone rang. 'Excuse me, Graham.' He frowned. 'I said I wasn't to be disturbed. Oh! Put her through.' His hand over the mouthpiece, he issued a brief message to Graham.

He wasn't aware of how much his face had revealed. He didn't care, hearing that clear, almost childish voice. He found it hard to speak.

'How marvellous to hear you. Where are you now?'

'Why didn't you tell me? Why on earth didn't you tell me?'

'What should I have told you?'

'You're looking for a cottage in Hailton. That's what you should have told me. Haven't I a right to know?' Her voice wasn't steady.

'How did you find out? I didn't tell anybody – '

'I live in a small place. We're all one family. A happy family . . . ' Her tone was bitter. 'I don't want to see you again. Stay with your own family.'

'I can't talk to you now. I want to. Very much.' He was astounded by the pure happiness which had descended upon him. 'I'll ring you back – '

'Just keep away from me. You've done enough damage. I don't want to see you again. That's all. Not ever again.' She hung up.

Stephen put the phone down. 'Sorry about that. A discarded mistress. I tried to let her down gently.'

Graham parodied a man-of-the-world smile. 'Spoken like a true gentleman.' He'd seen the change in Stephen's face: the bad temper had gone, the lines had been smoothed out, he'd looked almost touchingly young and naïve. Graham had no use for this knowledge at the moment, but stored it away for the future. He really wasn't planning to do Stephen down, but he'd reached the level where he wasted nothing.

'I could think again about this series,' Stephen said briskly. 'I might have been a bit hasty.'

'You'd better tell me what you think is wrong with it.' Graham spoke without heat, suddenly certain that he didn't have to push any more.

'Donny is wrong. Totally wrong. He just doesn't fit the part.'

'He'll get the ratings,' Graham said.

'The script gets the ratings, not the bloody cast. Anyway, I don't like him.'

'He's easy to work with. Learns his lines and turns up sober. What more do you want?'

'Oh yes, he's as close a facsimile of a human being as any actor ever can be. But he's the wrong size.'

'Is that of any consequence? It hasn't been so far.'

'He *looks* the wrong size to me. As if the factory had been tooled up for something bigger and they'd run out of material at the waist.'

'Ah, you have a keen incisive wit. But what does all that matter if the viewers like him? And he's not a bad actor.'

'He has improved lately. He only used to have two expressions. One was pure bewilderment – why had this woman locked the bedroom door and why was she breathing so heavily? The other was resignation – she's taken my pants off and I might as well go through with it. Now he's learned a third expression. Pure horror. As if he'd just wet himself.'

'All right, you've had your fun.' Graham smiled benignly. 'I say *I wish I'd said that* and you say *You will, Graham, you will* . . . Donny's becoming too greedy anyway. And playing hard to get. But let's put that aside for the moment. You know what I really want.'

Stephen laughed. 'Right now, not my considered opinion of the series. You want me to get things moving.'

'That's it.' Graham leaned back in his armchair, pulled out a packet of black shag tobacco and a packet of cigarette papers from the pocket of his Savile Row suit and rolled himself a cigarette with one hand. 'I've been speculating about what *you* want.'

'What would you like me to say? Axminster carpet instead of blue nylon? Or whatever the hell it is. A mahogany desk and a Regency casting couch?'

'You're too clever for me,' Graham said mildly. He lit a pencil-slim cigarette with a Dorchester Hotel book of matches. He'd never owned a lighter or bought a box of matches. 'But I think that you've been getting restless lately.' His tone hardened. 'You've heard about the Chairman?'

'I was very distressed. So sudden! Poor old chap. It's only a matter of days.'

Graham smiled. 'The company won't be the same without him. We shall not see his like again.'

'I did see it coming,' Stephen said. 'But I've done a certain amount of planning.'

'Fine.' Graham stood up. 'We'll talk about it soon.' He went to the door.

'We've got to play it by ear,' Stephen said, a little uneasily.

'Of course.' Graham lowered his voice. 'But stay with me. Don't travel too much. Stay where it's all going on.' He went out.

Instinct more than conscious deduction – and self-interest too – had prompted his warning. The carriage, one might say, had been driven away hell-for-leather from the Old Grange. But even as the door closed behind Graham, Stephen was already setting up absolutely valid professional reasons for visiting Charbury in the near future. He knew very well – he kept spelling it out incredulously and joyfully to himself – that if Robin really hadn't wanted to see him again she quite simply wouldn't have phoned him. And he wasn't really surprised that she'd somehow been informed of his looking for a cottage in Hailton. Whatever he did that affected her she'd always find out without even trying. The wind would tell her, or a mynah bird in a pet shop, or a scrap of paper in a bottle swept in by the tide. This is one of the few perquisites of the servants of love.

Stephen was carried along by an authentic exaltation for the rest of the day, and on his return home was so unwontedly and benignly mild that Jean became suspicious and edgy and the morning after went to her doctor for a prescription for the tranquillizers she'd abstained from for five weeks. It didn't help that, when she complained on going to bed of extreme nervous fatigue, he said placidly that he felt that way too and there was only one cure for it. And he fell asleep almost immediately, leaving her gloweringly awake. What she couldn't get over, what after half an hour sent her downstairs to heat herself a cup of milk and smoke three cigarettes and swallow two aspirins, was that the expression on his sleeping face wasn't, as usual, one of fierce resistance, of reluctant compliance to superior force. His expression was saying: *A fair cop, Guv'nor, I'll come quietly.* And it was absolutely out of character, it wasn't the man she'd married.

After she'd phoned Stephen, Robin sat by the bed for a while, as much taken over by exaltation as Stephen was. (It's even possible that she sensed this.) Remembering that harsh voice wasn't the same as actually hearing it. The words she had used and the words he had used were of no consequence. If they'd each recited from the telephone directory it wouldn't have changed anything. They'd not been in touch with each other for over nine months: neither of them had been in any danger of dying of a broken heart, but the separation had been hard to bear. Robin's exaltation, however, resembled Stephen's only in degree. She wasn't carried along by it, she was stunned by it. But anaesthetize would be a better word. Better still would be the phrase from the days of laughing-gas: she was experiencing *la belle indifférence.* The large oak four-poster bed with the plum canopy, the pink fitted carpet which was now overdue for replacement, the pink, blue and green flowered wallpaper which was supposed to look Victorian but never really had done, the solid oak bedroom furniture which she more and more frequently felt looked too damned solid, now looked perfect to her.

And then she ascended. The room was more than perfect. The room was full of light and she was part of the world of light. It was no longer important that she was a middle-aged matron, flesh and blood and in the end a handful of dust: she didn't feel that she could ever be sad again, and all the tears had been wiped away. *There must be something better than this*, her uncle Alec had said to her after the death of his son Tim in action on D-Day. She'd understood what he'd meant: he was trying not to mourn as the pagans mourn, having no hope. It wasn't the same, but the words fitted what she felt. What she had now, after hearing Stephen's voice again, was something better. In the garden that morning she'd noticed with pleasure that the snowdrops and the cherry and the saxifrage were in bloom, but had found herself impatient for the summer flowers, impatient in particular for roses. And now she had roses. She'd more and more recently thought of her bedroom as being too big. Now she was aware that it was exactly the right size, that it had been waiting to contain the light.

Unlike Stephen, she wasn't making any plans, except that she'd made an appointment with Petronella's headmistress in the afternoon and had promised to go to the Hailton Players Club Night with her friend Moira Villendam, who was coming to her for a snack beforehand. She was certain that her governance of her own life had once again been firmly established and she looked forward even to meeting Petronella's headmistress. And she'd meant what she'd said to Stephen. Naturally it hadn't mattered what she'd said: but naturally she'd also been absolutely sincere. *La belle indifférence* wouldn't be so described if it couldn't without straining accommodate such contradictions.

Joan the daily help, a grey-haired woman in her mid-fifties, came into the room as Robin got off the bed. 'Oh, you're there, Mrs Lendrick,' she said in a tone almost of admonition. 'That washing-machine's flooding. You haven't had it five minutes.'

'I'll have a look at it,' Robin said.

'Mind, considering what they charge for repairs, more than one repair and it's cheaper to buy a new one.'

'I'm sure you're right,' Robin said. She followed Joan

downstairs, not taking in her breathless blow-by-blow analysis of the washing-machine breakdown. She'd hear it all again anyway when they reached the laundry, and once again from the repairman. She didn't care what had happened to the washing-machine. She didn't even care whether Joan had been listening in to her phone conversation from downstairs, which from her manner as she came into the bedroom she strongly suspected she had.

Joan, a childless widow, lived in one of the few small houses in Throstlehill which hadn't yet been gentrified. She'd been born in Hailton, as her parents had. There weren't many people she didn't know in Hailton, and there weren't many people she didn't know all about. And what she didn't know she'd guess with surprisingly sophisticated accuracy. She knew all about Robin and Stephen's affair and all about Clive too. Now she'd know still more.

There was nothing to be done about it. Robin was right not to care. Still, what had happened to her was what had happened when nitrous oxide was first discovered. At laughing-gas parties people who fell over the furniture or down a flight of stairs or who even broke their limbs didn't realize that they were hurt. Not at the time. Not at the time.

Mirraton, the suburb of Charbury where Norman and Ruth lived, stood on a windswept plateau a thousand feet above sea level, with a view of the city to the south as far as Town Hall Square and a view to the north of a patchwork of steeply sloping fields and a scattering of stone cottages. Once it had been what is called a good address, but even before the Second World War the up-and-coming and the already arrived had begun to move slowly out of the city to places like Burley-in-Wharfedale, Bingley, Baildon, Ilkley and Hailton.

Ruth and Norman's flat was on the ground floor of a large stone house built in the 1900s to the specification of a successful wool merchant. It was square, solid and built to last, with well-kept lawns bordered with laurel. Like all the other large houses in the district it was a family house but would never now be a family house again. The parade had passed by for Mirraton and had passed by for Charbury. But there was still a sense of space and freedom and on a clear day in the right place a view almost as far as Harrogate. And the steep main road from the city was broad and straight and had about it a sense almost of triumph. Mirraton wasn't what it had been, but essentially there was nothing mean or cramped about it, and the present, except for a new housing estate to the south and two new supermarkets, didn't seem to have much power over it: there was always a feeling there that time had stopped, not even before 1939 but before 1914. Ruth and Norman didn't feel this, but Clive always did, though he didn't talk about it.

At a quarter to seven that evening in Ruth's bedroom as he and Ruth emerged smoothly and simultaneously from sleep after love, this thought was in fact in his mind. Though it wasn't really a thought, but a contentment: for a second on waking he hadn't known where he was or when it was, then had realized it was a sunset and there was no more pressure and he was with Ruth and it was Wednesday. They played their relationship by ear and it would have been diminished and cheapened by too unvarying a routine. Clive wasn't always free on a Wednesday in any case. But *cinq à sept* on a Wednesday was what suited them best.

Clive was more at home in Ruth's bedroom than he was in his own at Tower House. He virtually never visited what was now Robin's room. He hadn't given it any serious consideration, but there was a point when, soon after his forty-seventh birthday party, he'd turned against the room. His own bedroom was comfortable and well furnished, redecorated to his taste, and there was a new Dunlopillo mattress. But it never was quite the refuge which Ruth's room was. The straw matting and the pink nylon rugs, one each side of the bed, were in themselves the visual equivalent to him of Scotch with raspberry syrup or kippers with custard. Then there were the two scarlet bookcases, the scarlet plastic quilting on the bed-head, the pink dressing-table and chest of drawers and wardrobe and pelmet and the tangerine curtains: as he awoke he took it all in and was revived and supported by it, as he had been since first she took him to bed there.

Ruth sat up in bed and took a cigarette from the bedside table. 'I feel better after my sleep,' she said.

'I always feel better when I'm with you.' He stretched luxuriously. A spring in the mattress had broken loose and would at any moment scratch him, but in a strange way he didn't mind. The room made no demands upon him. It was on his side. When he came to think of it, no one had ever hurt him there.

'You're always nice to me,' she said. 'I don't think that you know how to be unkind.'

He ran his hand lightly over her breasts; their soft amplitude never failed to both excite and soothe him. 'I might have to learn in the very near future,' he said. 'Petronella is misbehaving. She's in trouble, in fact. Not deep trouble – she's just being damned silly. She thinks she can do just whatever she likes.'

'That's how it is with all teenagers,' she said comfortably.

'Christ, that isn't how it was with me! At her age I wasn't causing any trouble. Too busy swotting for the Matric. Wasn't much older than her when I learned all about the Sten gun. Not that there was very much to learn. It was rather a primitive weapon.'

She pushed the bedclothes down to uncover his belly and the long slanting scar from his shrapnel wound. 'Ah, but you've been through hell,' she said affectionately, stroking the scar. 'I don't see what it has to do with Petronella.'

'Well, she's turning so sodding awkward. I can't fathom what she's grumbling about most of the time. The trouble is these days that kids don't hear the word No very often. Even at St Perpetua's. I never heard anything else. Whatever you wanted to do when I was young, it was safe to assume you weren't allowed to do it.'

93

Her hand left the shrapnel scar and rested on his cheek briefly. 'Go on. Say they don't know they're born. What's she been doing, anyway? Dope?'

'God, no! Though I wouldn't be surprised if she's sampled the odd reefer. As far as I can see, she's not doing a stroke of work. And to make it worse, getting into everybody's hair. The Naughtiest Girl in the Fifth. Or rather the Sixth.'

'What's the problem, then? She's not pregnant, is she?'

'I hadn't thought about that. Now you've got me worried.'

'Like hell I have! Though you wouldn't like to be a grandfather. It'd be terribly ageing.'

'I don't know,' he said as if he hadn't heard her. 'Things are running away. And Robin's not herself. Petronella's not as she used to be.'

'No one is, darling.' She stubbed out her cigarette. 'Who did Robin use to be?'

'Nothing's the same, that's all. It was better during the War. No one got told they could do what the hell they wanted. Everything was clear. There were rules, and they stayed the same . . . '

'Yes, my pet.' She pushed the bedclothes further down. 'Do you think you could relax? Your face is all furrowed up. That doesn't please me. I like you to be happy and not give a damn.' She kissed him on the mouth, then on the shrapnel scar.

'I want things to make more sense,' he said. 'I want things to slow down . . . ' His voice trailed away.

'Don't talk,' she said. 'Relax. You don't have to do anything.' Her voice sank to a whisper. 'I'm not going to talk any more.'

Some fourteen minutes after there was a hoarse, ravished and sustained moan from Clive, descending into a kind of whimper. It wasn't all that different from the noises he'd made when the first shock of his shrapnel wound had worn off. (For the first sensation of a battle wound is a heavy blow, not sharp pain.) But of course he returned from his journey into another dimension, with the room still on his side and all tension and worry obliterated. And ahead of him lay an evening of temperate, simple but above all concrete pleasures – a shower, a stiff drink taken slowly, a good coarse garlicky pâté, fillet steak and salad and a bottle of Nuits-Saint-Georges – which they'd appreciate at its very high worth without feeling obliged to rhapsodize about it. And they'd listen to her new Mozart recording and he'd tell her everything that was on his mind. What he didn't tell her she'd make her own suppositions about, and they wouldn't be far off the mark. He didn't mention Donald. He didn't even think about him.

Donald at half-past nine, about to enter the new multi-storey car park just off Town Hall Square, was especially depressed and irritated precisely because he hadn't been able to forget about Clive. And though he wasn't unduly sensitive to his surroundings, the car park itself did nothing to lighten his spirits. Its concrete was already dingy and because of the empty space at window level on each floor – pierced by astoundingly few supporting uprights – its intimidating and graceless bulk seemed also dangerously unsubstantial. The walls by the lift were livid with graffiti and the lift smelled of urine.

He hadn't been able to forget about Clive because he hadn't been allowed to. Everyone at the Federation meeting, it seemed to him, had asked about Clive, had missed Clive. And it had been increasingly evident to him as the evening wore on that, as far as the majority of people in the wool trade were concerned, he and Clive were a double date and he was the plain one with spots and a home-made dress which dipped at the hem. And as Clive had prophesied, Seth and his mates had it all fixed beforehand. Donald could have saved himself the trouble.

As he got out of the lift and approached his Ford Zodiac two men were suddenly sandwiching him. Both were large, beefy, dressed in neat dark suits, their lace-up black shoes as if newly shined. They could have been any age, from forty to fifty. They didn't have the appearance of thugs, but of policemen or NCOs or prison warders. They grabbed Donald's arms, pulled him off his feet and towards them, then slammed him against the car door. He wasn't hurt, but the breath was knocked out of him.

'You haven't done what you promised, Mr Lendrick,' the man on his left said. Like the other he had a large jowly face and short hair, but his face made some attempt to be jovial and the other's didn't.

'Who the hell are you?' Donald said, getting his breath back.

The man flicked his finger under Donald's septum. The pain was momentary but excruciating. 'I'm Gary Cooper.' He nodded in the direction of his companion. 'That's John Wayne.'

Donald reached for his wallet. 'Look, take my money – '

The man gestured impatiently. 'It's Mr Simmerton you owe money to,' he said. 'You have a week.' He nodded to the other: Donald's spectacles were whisked off and thrown on the floor. Gary Cooper trod on them; Donald heard them crunch underfoot.

'That's unfortunate,' Gary Cooper said. 'How ever will you be able to drive home?'

'We'll give him a lift,' said John Wayne. His voice was as jarringly creaking as Gary Cooper's was soft and smooth.

'There now,' said Gary Cooper. 'It'd be no trouble at all. We know where you live. A very nice area. Wish I could afford to live there.'

Donald looked at him dumbly. His liquid intake had been less than usual that day, and he'd taken every opportunity to relieve himself but he wasn't any longer in control of his bladder. He felt a warm trickle down his leg.

'You've got two children,' John Wayne said to Donald.

'Ah yes,' Gary Cooper said, kicking the fragments of Donald's spectacles away. 'You're a lucky man, Mr Lendrick.

Children are a great blessing. A great worry too. When I was a kid, I could go *anywhere*. My parents knew I'd be safe. Why?' He prodded Donald in the belly. 'Because I had the finest guardian in the world.' He paused dramatically. '*The public hangman.*'

'Are you threatening me?' Donald managed to say.

Gary Cooper laughed. 'Don't know. what you mean.'

'Why don't you go to the police?' John Wayne asked.

'You do that,' Gary Cooper said. 'We're sorry you slipped on the nasty greasy floor and broke your glasses, though.' He flicked Donald's septum again. 'Good night, Mr Lendrick.'

When they'd gone, Donald looked at the dark patch at his groin and the dark streak down his left trouser leg and slumped back against the car door, shaking uncontrollably. After five minutes, he pulled himself upright, unlocked the car door, buttoned his raincoat, then sat in the driver's seat, his head in his hands. Then he sat upright, took out his spare glasses from the glove-box, put them on and turned the ignition key. He'd stopped shaking now and his face had an expression which hadn't ever visited it before, an expression which, if his wife and children had seen it, would both have mystified and frightened them. Clive, or anyone with combat experience, would have identified it immediately. If Gary Cooper and John Wayne had been in Donald's path as he drove his car out, he would have run them down, and reversed over them for good measure.

He made the journey back to Hailton in a little less than his usual twenty-three minutes, repressing a strong impulse to put his foot down on the throttle, wanting for a split second to bring fear to others, hating everyone else on the road and now feeling invulnerable, the big car a projectile aimed at Gary Cooper and John Wayne and most of all at Arthur Simmerton. The road to Hailton was broad and level with no sharp bends (although with two deceptively shallow ones), running parallel with the river along the valley, until within a mile of Hailton High Street it crossed the river and then rose gently and levelled out again. The landscape it passed through wasn't quite town and wasn't quite country, but town and country were at ease with each other and there was a sense of freshness and greenness and quietness.

Donald's house stood in a new housing estate at the top of the rise. The estate stood well back from the main road, the noise of the traffic cut off by the older buildings on the verge and the fields behind them. The house was red brick and its style was described by the builders as Georgian. The large window at the left had white shutters which were no more used than the small balcony above it was used. There was a red brick wall with a wrought-iron gate dividing the front garden from the back garden. The front was unfenced. There was a double garage with a narrow passage between it and the house. From the back there was a view of the river. It wasn't a bad-looking house, but its appearance was somehow two-dimensional. The five other houses in the cul-de-sac all looked exactly like it.

Donald was the house's first owner: he and Linda had seen it last summer, had immediately liked it and had immediately bought it. It was their third house since their marriage; the parquet had developed a ripple and they'd had trouble with the plumbing, but they were still delighted with the house. Unlike Clive and Robin, Donald and Linda preferred the new, wanted change, wanted to keep abreast of the times (though their fundamental moral values remained uncompromisingly non-permissive).

Now, putting the car away and despite his fatigue making the extra effort and reversing it into the garage as always, Donald was glad to be home with Linda and his children. The killer's cold exultation had left his face. But the anger was still there.

Linda opened the door to him and kissed him warmly.

'You look tired, darling.'

'It hasn't been a good day. I'll have a shower and go to bed early.'

'You do that, love.' She gestured at his spectacles. 'What happened to the others?'

'Dropped them going out after the meeting and some fool put his big foot on them.'

'That'll cost you,' she said.

'Every damned thing does these days,' he said. He turned to go upstairs.

'I nearly forgot,' she said. 'Bruce Kelvedon phoned. Says it's important.'

'It'll wait till I've had my shower,' he said. 'He's just another shareholder and not the biggest one either.'

After his shower, clean and refreshed and in clean pyjamas and dressing-gown, he phoned Bruce from the bedroom, comfortable and relaxed at last, lying on top of the king-sized bed propped up by four pillows.

'Bruce? What's so damned urgent that it won't keep until tomorrow?'

Bruce laughed. 'I should have thought that none of your present problems will be any the better for keeping.'

'What business is it of yours? And what the hell do you know about it, anyway?'

Bruce laughed again and named the exact figures of his debt to Arthur Simmerton and his bank overdraft.

'Jesus!' Donald said. 'Christ Almighty!' He could hardly speak for anger. 'You fucking bastard! What the bloody hell are you up to?'

'It isn't like you to use bad language, Donald.' Bruce still sounded amused. 'Besides, I want to help you. People like Arthur Simmerton really can be very persistent. Far more persistent than even the bank.'

'Yes,' Donald said. 'He *is* persistent.'

'Don't worry about him, old chap. He's a primitive organism. Very easy to deal with.' He paused. 'I think you and I should fix an appointment.'

'I think we should.' The anger had gone now and his brain

had never been so clear.

'Tomorrow at my place. Six. OK?'

'OK,' Donald said. 'You're still a fucking bastard.'

He hung up and went downstairs for a drink, feeling rowdily cheerful. For no good reason he felt that he was no longer the plain partner in the double date.

Eight

At the moment that Donald was phoning Bruce, Norman was sitting in Desmond's Club in Charbury and his friend Monty had just joined him. He wasn't drunk but he was halfway through his third large brandy and dry ginger and his focus was alternately frighteningly sharp and frighteningly fuzzy. He could have put up with one or the other, but not both in rapid succession.

Now he saw Monty's well-disciplined thick silver grey hair, his pink closely shaven banker's face, his dark brown blazer and contrasting fawn slacks, his maroon and green brushed cotton shirt and plain green woollen tie and maroon, green and chocolate Paisley snuff handkerchief with the feeling that it was all too much for him, that Monty was pushing too hard, he looked too damned distinguished. And he could smell the Eau de Portugal on his hair, too, and the faintly antiseptic smell of Wright's Coal Tar soap, and the cloying sweetness of his American pipe tobacco, brought back from his last trip to Fire Island. He felt that the mural – pink naked cherubim hotly pursued by huge pink angels in see-through robes – was also too much for him. He didn't feel at home any more in the long room with the long bar, he didn't trust the proprietor Desmond, tall, willowy and hatchet-faced, dapper in a pale green mohair suit and dark green suede shoes, moving among his customers now with a word or a kiss or a quick pat on the head or buttocks according to his or their inclinations. The long room was too long, there were too many people in it and there were too many musky colognes. Norman preferred sharper, lighter and lemony colognes like Eau Sauvage.

A slim, doe-eyed young Pakistani came into the room,

caught sight of Monty and smiled at him dazzlingly. Monty blew him a kiss.

'I haven't seen him before,' Norman said, suddenly brightening.

'Neither have I.' Monty grinned. 'The young can't resist me. I'm the archetypal father figure.' It was true: he looked his age of sixty, but he also was cheerfully content to be that age.

'That's not for me,' Norman said sadly. 'I've always been the wrong age – too young or too bloody old.'

'My dear, you shouldn't think about it. Just be yourself.'

'And who's myself?' Norman saw things fuzzily now, but it wasn't a pleasant softening of rough edges but rather as if line and colour and sound were all bleary and deliquescent.

Monty patted his knee. 'A most intelligent and sensitive person who's made an absolutely marvellous adjustment to life. And very attractive too. That suede jacket really suits you. Not butch, but terribly masculine.'

'That's sweet of you.' Norman visibly preened himself. Monty always said the right thing. Monty was always reassuring. Monty never hurt his feelings. Monty never had more than a one-night stand with anyone, no matter how appealing; but he stayed friends with them afterwards. That was his special gift: to be promiscuous and yet not to use people. His own one night stand had been the consequence of a serious tiff with Gary; afterwards he'd been able to see it in perspective, chiefly because Monty at breakfast had given him exactly the right advice.

'And that red cravat is perfect,' Monty said. He took a sip of his gin and bitters. 'I personally couldn't wear it – too young and dashing for me. But you can more than get away with it.' He looked at Norman's glass. 'Another tincture?'

Norman nodded. Monty strolled over to the bar. Like Desmond he greeted people with a brief word or gesture of recognition or a brief caress: unlike Desmond, the impression was that he was in the bosom of his much-loved family.

Norman lit a Gauloise Bleu: suddenly he was back to normal and able to put Gary and himself in perspective. Colour and line and sound weren't bleary any longer, he was relaxing enjoyably and sensibly. And the smell of the various colognes was now to him as the smell of cordite is to the soldier. He was himself again and prepared to enjoy himself, to let go amongst his own people. Monty would ask from him nothing but his friendship: there'd be no ecstasy but there'd also be no pain.

Gary and Miriam Cothill and her accountant Cyril were at that moment having coffee and liqueurs at the Benissimo, a new Italian restaurant in a bow-fronted Victorian building off Parliament Street in Harrogate. Gary had enjoyed his fried whitebait and Scalappa Marsala and had asked for a bottle of Pellegrino so that it was absolutely apparent that he was taking it easy with the wine. Now he and Miriam Cothill were sipping Strega, Cyril was sipping Scotch.

He always had enjoyed Harrogate and the gentle and civilized country around it, its solid and cheerful elegance and the open spaces like the Stray and the Valley Gardens and Harlow Moor which had been planned to give pleasure but at the same time seemed to have occurred spontaneously and to have decided their own shape. And it was high enough above sea level for the air never to be less than bracing, but it wasn't so high as to be windswept and bleak: he didn't suffer from what Norman called the Wuthering Heights syndrome, he had no desire to defy the elements. Part of the attraction which Miriam Cothill had for him was that she had a big house near Harrogate; he wondered rather peevishly why he'd never been invited there, but decided to take it easy, as he'd taken the wine.

He was well content with the restaurant in any case, apart from the food. For one thing, the shocking pink and pale fawn of the brand-new décor was an almost exact match for his button-down silk shirt, and the hearts in the tie Norman had given him. And he knew that he looked especially young in contrast to Cyril, a middle-aged man in a crumpled dark grey suit, dark grey tie with an extraordinarily small knot, and crumpled red face with broken veins and small shrewd eyes. Miriam Cothill, forty-three and fresh from a week at a health farm, still had about her an aura of saunas and massage, sunray lamps and deep-pore cleansing, was still holding age back, as it were, with almost contemptuous ease; but her large blue eyes were hungry whenever she looked at Gary, her rather too thin hand kept darting across to his wrist. Gary in fact felt curiously at home with her: small, slim and fair with features which only just missed being meagre, she was, though not boyish, not too cloyingly feminine. And her sheer energy and almost feverish animation fascinated him. She didn't have beauty: but her face didn't bore him.

He answered Cyril's questions automatically, realizing that Cyril was, after all, only an employee. And the motive behind his questions was merely to show his employer that he didn't miss a trick.

'There's only one more minor point,' Cyril said. 'I'm not entirely happy about some aspects of your investments – '

Miriam Cothill's hand chopped down suddenly. 'No, Cyril. The boy's a daring young entrepreneur, for Christ's sake, not a geriatric dividend-drawer. Let's get down to business.' Her hand now rested briefly on Gary's hand instead of his sleeve. It was very hot, almost feverish; he found himself not minding.

'Cyril's only doing his job,' he said, and smiled charmingly at him. One couldn't have too many friends. 'In his shoes I'd be very careful with your money too. But I agree with you. Let's get down to business.'

'You can have the money,' she said. 'But the shop has to be called *Gary's*.'

'It's a frightful name,' he said. 'Real council house. Fractionally better than Clint or Wayne, but only fractionally.'

'It's fine for the sort of shop you're going to have. It's so *awful* that it has shock value. It's a bit camp, too. Not chi-chi. Camp.' She grinned at him, now much younger, even gamine. 'Like that dreadful tie. And that even more dreadful display hanky. It's enjoyable, it has much the same taste as zabaglione and Strega.'

'The question is whether there's the money in Hailton,' Cyril said heavily.

'Oh, yes,' Miriam Cothill said. 'More than there is in the South. They still keep it in their old socks and under the mattress.'

'We'll have to charm it out of them,' Gary said. 'But not with rubbish, not with trendy tat.'

'You're on my wavelength,' Miriam Cothill said.

Gary kissed her hand, judging that the moment had come to risk a little harmless gallantry. 'It'll be a pleasure to work with you,' he said, deepening his voice so that it was more than usually resonant and, he hoped, sincere.

'Don't think it won't be work, Gary,' Miriam Cothill said sharply. 'I'm a very tough lady.'

'That's rather frightening, Miriam,' Gary said lightly. But he wasn't really frightened and she knew that he wasn't. Gary was as tough and self-contained as she was and as coldly sensual. He might well at his age still be sentimental about friendship, but he'd grow out of that. And he was definitely an acquisition which would prove her good taste and which would cause envy among most of the women of her acquaintance and not a few of the men. He wouldn't be cheap, but he was well within her means. Of course he was AC/DC, she reflected, and a thorough shit into the bargain: but that curly chestnut hair and choirboy face and rather beautiful voice in themselves made him worth buying. And he belonged entirely to the material world; he was cheerful, frivolous and essentially decadent and for a while anyway, just her cup of tea or, rather, rainbow cocktail. She smiled at him briefly, the smile saying it all, and gestured to the waiter for the bill.

Gary went home to Hailton in his Morris Minor Traveller,

very happy about being bought and rather surprised by his realization that if it came to it he certainly wouldn't throw Miriam out of his bed. He wasn't madly eager about it and, he thought soberly, if he'd misread her signals he wouldn't push it. But he was rather surprised to find himself acknowledging that the memories of his two heterosexual couplings in his teens were good ones. They'd been pushed away in the back of a cupboard for a long time, tarnished and apparently valueless; but now they were taken into the light, so to speak, and polished up, he could perceive that they were solid silver. They weren't at all sophisticated and they'd been brief and even primitive but there was no argument about the satisfaction afterwards and the boisterous glow which he now experienced when he remembered them.

He'd never confided his heterosexual experiences to Norman: he always played his cards pretty closely to his chest. But at the moment when Gary was remembering what had happened in the bushes in Roundhay Park and in the back seat of a borrowed Austin 12 behind a Leeds dance hall respectively, Norman at Desmond's Club was beginning his fifth large brandy and dry ginger and his words were keeping upright only with difficulty, struggling painfully and slowly up a steep, icy hill, clutching the handrail on the verge of the pavement. Maybe there was actually an image like this somewhere in his mind, though the new central heating in the crowded room was working all too well and it was mild outside. Norman, quite undeservedly, and certainly through no wish of his own, was now in a cold country on a cold day. So were Gary and Miriam, but they were natives of that country. Norman had, so to speak, been deported there.

'It's quite understandable for the boy to want to better himself,' he said to Monty, lighting another Gauloise.

Monty patted his hand. 'Most natural thing in the world, old chap. You wouldn't respect him very much if he didn't.'

'I'd have helped him, you know.' Norman nodded owlishly.

'Yes, indeed I would. Made him the offer. I wouldn't have gone back on it.' His tone became angry. 'I'm not that sort of man. My word is my bond.' He was as if defending himself against a fierce attack.

'Who's saying otherwise? But it's just as well, old chap. Make friends of those you go into business with, but don't go into business with friends. Relations are even worse.'

'The woman's Miriam Cothill. A widow, lives near Harrogate. I gather she's rich.'

Monty frowned and sucked his pipe rather noisily for a moment as if the process would somehow refresh his memory. 'Never met her. Name rings a bell, though. Wait.' He sucked his pipe again, then took it out of his mouth and rubbed the bowl lightly against his nose. He then took it away from his nose and scrutinized it like a Roman soothsayer inspecting the entrails of a sacrificial beast. 'Fortyish. In property. And other things. Very hard. Unwomanly, in fact. I'd say that she was diversifying now. The property boom won't last for ever.'

'Does she have children?' He didn't know why he'd asked this.

'A son no one ever sees. He's got two heads or no John Thomas or no nose and eyes – you take your choice. Something horribly wrong with him anyway. So I've heard.'

Norman was suddenly sober. 'Does she like young men?'

Monty went through the pipe performance again. 'I hear that she has healthy appetites. Not that I move in the same circles. Dear me, no. I'm content to be the faithful steward of my modest inheritance. At the end of the day, as long as there's enough for a decent burial and a ham tea and a few drinks for my friends – well, I shan't complain. Why should I wear myself out making money for my boozy sod of a nephew to squander?' He grinned.

He didn't for one moment expect Norman to believe him: Norman was fully aware of how much property he owned, how little of it was rent-controlled, how many prime sites he had and, most important of all, how many friends he had at the Town Hall. He was, in fact, the archetypal West Riding warm man.

'Yes, Monty,' Norman said. 'Avarice is a dreadful thing. But Mrs Cothill likes young men.'

'Only young men who make her money. I doubt if she's capable of passion for its own sake.' Monty patted Norman's hand. 'But why worry? Gary isn't that sort of a boy. Believe me, dear old chum, he's in no danger.'

'Of course, *he* isn't in any danger,' Norman said bitterly. 'If anyone ever hurt him it's a long time ago. And it wasn't a man.'

Monty grinned. 'Oh, the good old Oedipus complex. My mother made me a homosexual. Or my father didn't understand me. Or the whole family didn't understand me.'

'I've heard it.' Norman's voice was flat. 'It's a load of rubbish. My mother and father, my bloody brothers are so normal and understanding that they make me want to puke. And I didn't go to boarding school either.'

'I went to boarding school,' Monty said. 'Never had such a good time before or since. Sometimes I dream I've gone back there and I wake up with a big smile.' He chuckled. It was a mellow, practised chuckle. 'I was everybody's darling. Even the dear old Head would touch me up from time to time.'

'How nice for you,' Norman said. His tone was acid. 'Nothing disturbs you very much, does it Monty? You're a real philosopher.'

'I don't let anything disturb me,' Monty said. 'Once *you* didn't, Norman dear. You were a great enigma, weren't you? You'd come here occasionally and sit around with a Dubonnet, and flirt a little, then suddenly go off home to Ruth. We all used to wonder what the hell you came for.'

'Maybe I did myself. But it was better than it is now. I don't like it now.' His face convulsed. 'Why the hell should I let that fucking little gold-digger get under my skin?'

'Everything has to be paid for.' Monty caught Desmond's eye, pointed to the drinks and gave Desmond a tight little smile. 'But you *did* have what you paid for. You must have known it wouldn't be cheap.'

'I can't be bothered,' Norman said, as if he hadn't heard. 'I can't be bothered to work it all out. Haven't got the energy.' He hadn't the energy now, he thought, but only last spring he'd had the energy. He'd been able to work it all out and work it out without panic. Or perhaps he'd heard a warning, a warning in good time. If the offer of the partnership in Surrey hadn't come up there'd have been something else coming up: all that had mattered had been the decision to go.

'I think that you should make the decision just the same,' Monty said. 'Just look at the situation coolly. Don't get too emotional. Gary's very charming and very pretty but – ' he waved his hand round the room as if offering Norman a choice – 'he's not the only young man in the world.' He stood up. 'Excuse me a moment.'

'That isn't any help,' Norman said, half to himself. He rubbed his smarting eyes: despite the electric fan which had just started up, the room was too smoky and was becoming oppressively warm. 'It's no help at all,' he said to Monty's empty chair. 'I can't be sensible.' He saw a crew-cropped young man in a leather jacket and combat boots looking at him curiously, noting his wafer-thin gold watch and heavy gold identity bracelet, new suede jacket and silk cravat, and then smiling at him boldly. He looked away from the young man and down at the table and tried to think nothing, to feel nothing, to be absolutely still, and was on the way to stillness and then heard Monty's voice and saw the empty chair filled.

'Ah, you've put on your thinking-cap, my dear,' Monty said with approval. 'As I say, there are other young men in the world.' He took another sip of gin and bitters. 'And, I may add, other places.'

Norman finished his brandy and dry ginger at a gulp and then stared at the new glass of brandy which had just appeared. 'Other places? I mightn't want to go there.'

'Would Ruth go with you? That might be important.'

Norman laughed. 'Ruth? She'll never leave this district. Not as long as Clive is there. They have a very cosy arrangement.'

'So you've often told me,' Monty said rather distastefully. 'Personally I've observed that these cosy arrangements always blow up sooner or later.'

Norman found himself slightly irritated. 'It won't blow up. Everyone's perfectly happy.' He took a sip of the neat brandy and then put the glass down: he felt as if the alcohol were playing cat-and-mouse with him, picking him up, shaking him, dropping him, letting him run, bringing him back from comparative sobriety to be shaken again.

'You're deceiving yourself,' Monty said. He looked round the room again, glanced at the young Pakistani, then looked Norman full in the face, his expression now positively magisterial. 'Believe me, those people don't care about you. Break loose. *Get out of it.*'

'I'm going home,' Norman said. He stood up, swaying slightly. Things were beginning to blur again.

'I'll give you a lift,' Monty said, draining his glass.

'It's out of your way. I'll get a cab.'

'Don't argue, old thing. I'll give you a lift.' Monty took his hand. It was a warm, strong hand and Norman was glad of it.

Outside in the fresh air it was all sharply in focus again. The narrow cobbled street into which they emerged had been a street of character once, within fifteen minutes' walk of Town Hall Square, with a gunsmith, a bespoke shoemaker and shirtmaker and two tailors of Savile Row standards. But a new shopping centre had cut off easy access to the city at one end and at the other end were huge gaps where the bulldozers had been at work, apparently at random, since the late Fifties. The shops were all boarded up now, everyone had gone away and wouldn't come back. The street was a Victorian development in local stone, austere for its period and with unusually large windows on the upper floors but with its austerity relieved by its carved pediments and pierced on each side by four broad alleys each leading to cobbled courtyards. The parapets appeared somehow light and graceful, their purpose purely decorative. Norman took it all in and then rejected it, fixing his eyes on Monty's car, parked near to the tall wire fence at the back of the huge concrete bulk of the shopping centre.

Monty's car was a 1939 Rover 14 Sports Saloon, in pristine condition, staid and stolid but not high and boxy, with a running-board and curious wings which were cycle-type in outline but fixed, as if the designer had intended it to be a real sports car but had changed his mind. Monty kept it out of sentiment – it had been his father's personal car rather than the firm's Rolls-Royce – and out of snobbery: everyone he knew now had a Jaguar or a Mercedes or even a Ferrari or a Maserati but only he had a car like the Rover. It helped his image all the more because everyone was aware that he could have afforded any other car his heart desired. And inside, Norman felt with gratitude, there was a feeling of enormous security, of privileged comfort, the gleam of walnut and the smell of leather. One didn't merely sit in the Rover, one almost resided in it.

This, of course, was all illusion. He was indeed right to feel a sense of enormous security in the Rover, but only because Monty was a careful driver, never drank more than his limit and kept the car meticulously maintained. It was a good car, not of an inspired design but safely driveable within its limitations: it wasn't immune to disaster, but with Monty at the wheel it would get him safely home. And that was all. It was a car and not a residence, and he and Monty wouldn't stay there. Monty would have had a brief conversation with Desmond earlier, and when he'd dropped Norman would return to his large Victorian house near Central Park – once the family home – to await the arrival by taxi of the doe-eyed young Pakistani. Monty was aware of what Norman had once been aware of: get involved and you get hurt. The young Pakistani would go home by taxi in the morning, tired but happy, appreciably richer, and having lost nothing he hadn't lost before. And Monty would sit placidly in his ground-floor flat, brew himself another pot of coffee and browse through the *Yorkshire Post*. He would be alone and happy to be alone. He wouldn't be lonely. He found company of the kind he wanted when he needed it; and having enjoyed it would return to contented solitude.

Norman was now returning not to solitude but a shared life with Ruth. He kept his eyes half-closed during the journey, aware only of climbing, wanting only to rest. He didn't open his eyes fully until he got out. He was still seeing all too clearly, but now he could exclude the night and all strangers and the stony hills and the stony city and look straight ahead at the large square house that was his home because Ruth was there. And he could see that Clive's Mercedes was still there and was happy to see it there and found himself remembering the time when Clive had lived there, not of course as the third in a *ménage à trois* but very much part of the family. That was something nice to remember, he thought as he let himself into the large hall with the tiled floor and Victorian walnut table with a litter of mail, mostly brochures, on it, and the large stained-glass window with two knights jousting which might have been William Morris but wasn't.

Ruth was pouring Clive coffee when he entered the living-room. She'd had a spring-cleaning binge recently and the books in the two large bookcases had been sorted out and shelf-edged and the confusion of bric-à-brac on the tops of the bookcases sorted out too. And before Christmas she'd had the posters and pages ripped from newspapers thrown out and had got rid of all the old pictures too, and had the walls repapered in a blue lozenged pattern of multi-coloured exotic birds. And there was a new three-piece red and black studio couch. She hadn't got around to choosing new pictures yet, nor tidied the long deal table with the paints and brushes and various artists' materials on it, because part of the stuff was his – indeed, the living-room was their shared territory. The room wasn't as it would have been if he'd been the sole occupant; and indeed it was still rather unsure of its identity, neither a lively and harmonious whole, in good taste but effortlessly so, nor nonchalantly trendy, Bohemian in the best sense, cocking a snook at *Homes and Gardens* but still being more than just untidy. It didn't matter: he was at home there and there was a family life going on of which in a strange way he was part. He sat down gratefully in the armchair nearest the gas fire. The room was very warm, but he wanted warmth now, and could almost have wished for snow outside and a howlingly cold wind from the east.

Ruth kissed him. 'Coffee, Norman?'

'Lovely, darling. How are you, Clive?'

'Fine, old chap. We've just had a quiet evening. I forgot all about the bloody mill. You been anywhere interesting?'

'Here and there. Ended up at Desmond's Club.'

Clive looked mildly surprised. Norman wasn't in the least ashamed of being what he was, but he was rarely so forthcoming. 'They tell me that it's very amusing.'

'You'd be surprised who goes there,' Norman said, taking a cup of coffee from Ruth.

'Not any more,' Clive said. 'Nothing surprises me. Except that the country still staggers on, with the government and the councils spending public money as if there were no tomorrow.'

'Don't go into the old things ain't what they used to be act, darling,' Ruth said. She kissed his hand. 'You're tired, anyway.' She looked at Norman. 'Norman, you don't look so grand. Do you want some brandy? Or a Montezuma?'

'Maybe a Montezuma later.' Norman looked at her with gratitude: Montezumas as a nightcap were one of the bonds between them, small in one sense and hugely important in another: he'd never drunk one with anyone else. He stretched out his legs. 'I'll just unwind a bit. It's been one of those days . . .'

'I know the feeling.' Clive glanced at his watch. 'It's time I was off. I've got one of those days ahead of me tomorrow. My bloody brother's constructing even more disaster scenarios than usual. Can't manage for a moment without me.'

'He managed when you weren't there once,' Norman said. 'He did, he really did . . . ' He was surprised to find himself saying it and didn't know why he should say it.

'Ah, yes, he did,' Clive said. 'He certainly did. Had no bloody option. We've got other sales staff – ' His anger was mounting, but not at Norman. He checked himself abruptly. 'I really must go.' He kissed Ruth. 'I love you, darling.' He put his hand on Norman's shoulder. 'See you, Norman.'

Forty minutes later when they were sitting together with their Montezumas, Ruth asked gently: 'What's wrong, Norman?'

He took another sip from his mug. 'This is just right, darling,' he said. 'The cheap brandy is best. Brings out the taste of the chocolate.'

She disregarded this. 'What's wrong, Norman?'

'You mean I shouldn't have referred to the time when he bolted the coop and was our house guest?'

She shook her head impatiently. 'Why shouldn't you? He did live with me for over two months. Everybody knows it. Talk about it as much as you like.'

'I lived here too. Very much so.'

'Of course you did. No one ever proposed that you should go. Clive certainly didn't. He's very fond of you.'

'Fond. Fond.' He put out his hand as if physically pushing it away. 'It isn't what I need.'

'Oh God, what shall I do with you?' She came up beside him, and stroked his hair. 'It's Gary, isn't it?'

'*Bébé est vicioux – il aime les femmes* – it sticks in my mind.'

She moved back to the sofa and lit a cigarette. 'It doesn't make much difference, does it? I don't think it'll last, one way or another.'

He didn't answer her but sipped his Montezuma, the colour coming back to his cheeks. 'Monty gave me a lift tonight,' he said. 'Homely wisdom and pipemanship. He's got it all made,

114

you know.' He was silent again. She didn't answer him but, half smiling, shared his silence as an act of friendship. 'I don't want to be like that,' he said. 'Not that Monty hurts anyone.'

'I don't know much about him. Met him at some frightful musical function at Harrogate once. He's a patron of this, that and the other.'

Norman giggled. 'I know what he's patron of.' He drank his Montezuma and stood up. 'Well, it's me for my chaste couch.' He yawned. 'I feel better now I'm home.' He paused. 'Clive's a bit upset, isn't he?'

'As far as he ever allows himself to be. He just doesn't want trouble.'

'Stephen's trouble,' Norman said. 'Still, what will he do? It doesn't matter to you and Clive – ' He stopped. 'Sufficient unto the day is the evil thereof.' He kissed Ruth lightly. 'Good night, darling.'

'Good night,' she said, and pressed his hand to her breasts. 'Don't worry, dear old Norman – it'll be all right in the end.'

But though now she was tired – and wholesomely tired after love and a good meal and music – she stayed where she was on the sofa, thinking over Norman's words. And when she finally went to her room it was an hour before she got to sleep, and in dream after dream great shapeless beasts chased her and shapeless crumpled figures hemmed her in.

But Norman in his incredibly neat room – black and white, green and crimson, thick fitted carpet, all in apple-pie order, everything for comfort and nothing for effect, military rather than twee – switched on his electric blanket for ten minutes, switched it off, put on the all-cotton Marks and Spencers pyjamas he always preferred and was asleep almost immediately. If he had any dreams he wouldn't remember them on waking. He had now excluded the world outside completely and had pulled the new crimson velvet curtains firmly together on entering the room. There was everything that he needed within the confines of the flat and here he could come to no harm. He wasn't going out until morning and in the morning he'd be rested and have as much courage as he needed. He was alone and expected to be alone; but he wasn't lonely because Ruth was near. He would have found it perfect had Clive been in her room with her: but he was satisfied with what he'd got. Of course he was aware the instant before he fell asleep that his problem would still be there in the morning. But he was home and renewing his strength: Antoneus had his feet on the earth.

Don't think of him as a minor character. He was not a minor character to himself. There are no minor characters in this story; they're all involved with each other and, in varying degrees and in their different ways, pay a high price for this.

Nine

Two weeks later at eleven in the morning Stephen took the turning off the A1 for Wakefield and, eventually, Leeds, Bradford and Charbury. It was a bleak morning for spring, with a pale sun browbeaten by slate-grey clouds and rain on the way. The landscape was typically South Yorkshire, flat, featureless, disgruntled, with farmland with which one could never associate Harvest Festivals or rolling in the hay – or indeed any kind of jollity – and trees which one felt would give no shade or shelter, which were simply wood, the dryads not having gone away but never having been there. And the buildings were small and frowning, mostly in local stone and yet not belonging to the locality, squatters brazening it out. As a landscape its only virtue was that it was absolutely consistent. It was never in any way cheerful and positively preferred bad weather.

It didn't depress Stephen, but on the contrary lifted his spirits still further. There weren't many people around – a shapeless young woman tugging along a howling toddler to the Co-op, two men in overalls about to rupture themselves extricating a freezer cabinet from a van, an old woman outside the Post Office staring at her pension book as if she weren't entirely confident that her pension would be paid – but one and all, Stephen reflected, appeared as if they led lives which by his standards simply weren't worth living. He would have fun today and be paid for it: whatever fun ordinary people had, they'd have to pay for it and it would be mass-produced, tasteless and pawed over.

This thought was to him much as the contemplation of the sufferings of the damned in Hell was once supposed to be to the blessed in Heaven. It was really a form of *schadenfreude*. He wasn't a very nice man. Clive wasn't in the least like that. If ever it had occurred to him that the majority of people had a pretty lousy time of it, it wouldn't have caused him to miss any sleep, but he'd have felt sorry for them. He was, in short, kind, and kind instinctively.

What Stephen and Clive felt about ordinary people showed without them being aware of it. The result was that ordinary people and particularly waiters and doormen and shop assistants and taxi drivers dimly resented Stephen as a jumped-up nobody, but tended to fawn over Clive. Clive got rather better service than Stephen, even though Stephen habitually overtipped. Those who pocketed the tips weren't grateful for them, seeing them, quite rightly, as a measure of his contempt for menials.

Neither of them was thinking about each other as Stephen drove along the Wakefield road at a steady fifty. Clive, in fact, was alone in his office with a cup of coffee and a sheaf of new designs from Charley Horsmorden and had closed his eyes for a moment, feeling suddenly tired. This had been happening to him more and more often recently; at moments he'd feel as if his body had been emptied of strength. Stephen was wide awake and practical, all the facts and figures he'd need for the forthcoming meeting at Deira TV in a neat folder in his leather briefcase and, which was most important, in his head. His instructions from Saxon TV were to get much more from Deira TV than Saxon would give to Deira: he would for appearances' sake aim at this, settle for less, but get something from Deira which Saxon hadn't expected, but would be delighted to have. So everyone would be happy and he, Stephen, would proceed onwards and upwards. Of course there couldn't be a merger, but there were many ways in which they could co-operate, or at least agree to lay off each other.

He wasn't thinking about Robin: by and large he had a compartmentalized mind. He was in the Jaguar on the way to

Charbury now because some two months ago he'd started longing for Robin again, his memories of her becoming positively substantial and tangible; and she had taken over his dreams, always within touching distance but never touched. And Hailton was part of it, Hailton had become an enchanted place – a stormy sky over the moors and the lovers running towards each other, keeping time to surging background music as if taking part in a ballroom dancing contest. He could mock himself for being besotted by this vision, he could tell himself he was an idiot, he could tell himself that there was no future in it, he could remind himself again and again of his bright indefatigable little son, he could also grasp the fact that if he lost Jean he lost his son too.

Still Robin was there and that calm of hers, that halcyon stillness and that feeling he'd have with her of being a better person. He couldn't say precisely how he'd be better: at his age he wasn't about to become kind, generous, loving, unselfish, compassionate or even to feel that he ought to live for something outside of himself. But with Robin, though she certainly had never tried to reform him, certainly had never tried to inspire him to higher things, he'd always remembered in her company that higher things existed, had always had his youthful idealism reawakened, not entirely to her comfort.

What was taking him to Charbury, however, was a romantic impulse. He was Heathcliff running towards Cathy. And the romantic impulse had compelled him to enquire about a cottage in Hailton. The visit to Deira TV, the whole complicated deal and the possibility of other deals arising from it, was no more than an excuse to visit Yorkshire and see Robin again. To be valid as an excuse, however, the deal had to be feasible, had to be worth the expenditure of time on his visit, even if he'd never met Robin. So now in his suit from Huntsman's (a soft mid-grey with a tinge of blue and burnt amber, a new design from Lendrick Mills), made-to-measure shoes from Lobb's, and silk shirt and silk tie from Gieves and Hawkes, he was entirely the senior executive, senior and responsible and dependable, but with fire in his belly. Robin wasn't in the compartment of his mind which he'd be using with Deira TV. In fact, there weren't any human beings there at all. He didn't regard the three men he was about to meet as human beings, though he had personally met them all in the past on social terms and had been briefed on their backgrounds and idiosyncrasies. They were at the top of the heap, they had the authority to make decisions; but he didn't see them as real people, any more than they saw him as a real person. He would as soon leave them in a glow of it's-all-been-to-our-mutual-interest good fellowship than leave them feeling vaguely that they'd been screwed: but he didn't give a damn about any of them. He'd met too many people, there'd been too many deals. And all that this deal boiled down to was the allocation of areas of interest, as with gangsters in Chicago during the Roaring Twenties.

In this again he was different from Clive. Clive wasn't exactly a golden-hearted and trusting simpleton in business, was just as much of a thruster as Stephen was. But he nearly always made friends with those he did business with, he saw them as individual persons who bled when pricked and laughed when tickled, and he had the ability to leave even the hardest cases feeling that he hadn't done anything so sordid as sell them cloth for his personal profit, but had done them a great favour because he genuinely liked them.

Robin at eleven in the study of Tower House was going through what Stephen would have called the bourgeois ritual of a coffee morning. She was in fact rather enjoying herself. Mary Hardrup, thinner recently and even paler, was there, her eyes more restless than ever. She wasn't to be trusted, and she had a sharp tongue, but she knew all the scandal in Hailton before even Joan knew it, and one couldn't help but listen. Her sister-in-law Linda was there, looking surprisingly relaxed and, whenever she looked in Robin's direction, curiously triumphant. Fiona Sindram, on the other hand, was more subdued than ever she'd been, her red hair more orange than red, the spring gone from her figure. And Moira Villendam and her sister June Thomas, round-faced and placid, their hair greying and not giving a damn about it, were listening out of politeness to Linda's account of the new antacid, obtainable on prescription only, which had done such wonders for Donald's nervous dyspepsia whilst becoming more and more fascinated by Mary Hardrup's blow-by-blow account of the Hailton Young Conservatives' goings-on in the Municipal Park on Saturday at midnight. Mary Hardrup whispered the juiciest scandals but her whisper was a theatrical whisper, capable of reaching the back row of the gallery, let alone the corner of the study where she was sitting with Fiona Sindram.

'Naked,' Mary Hardrup whispered. 'Starkers. The whole lot of them.' She rattled off the names of the principal dryads and satyrs.

'He's simply not *sending* me the money,' Fiona Sindram said. 'He has the money to spend on his fancy bit, though – '

'It takes them that way at a certain age,' Robin said gravely. 'He'll come back, you'll see.'

'She's so cheap and *common*!' Fiona Sindram said. 'God knows, I'm broadminded. But she is the *end*. His partners don't like it. She's young enough to be his daughter.'

'He's the one who'll be sorry,' Robin said, listening at the same time to Mary Hardrup's terse yet somehow graphically detailed account of the open-air frolics of the Hailton Young Conservatives. It hadn't been very warm on Saturday night, indeed in this part of the world winter could hang around doggedly even well into May; but she found herself warmed for a moment at the thought of those wild leaping young bodies, had no wish that she'd joined them, but wished that when she'd been their age she could have felt the grass under her bare feet, that she too could have rejoiced in her youth.

'He won't be sorry,' Fiona Sindram said dejectedly. 'Men always get the best of it.'

And she was right, of course: the deserted wife got a lot of

121

sympathy, she was undeniably in the right, but the invitations dried up: a single man got them, but not a single woman.

'It's the way the world is,' Robin said. She drifted over to Mary Hardrup. 'More coffee, Mary?'

'Please,' Mary said. As usual she had somehow dominated the whole gathering: she was at the centre of it now, she had finished with the Hailton Young Conservatives and was deciding upon her next subject. 'Khaki, please, Robin. Just enough to colour it. And two spoonfuls.' She paused. 'Whenever I come here, I think what a lovely house this is. So spacious, yet so homey.'

'Far too spacious,' Robin said, refilling cups and then sitting casually opposite her. 'We don't need all these rooms. We've talked about selling it, actually.' They hadn't really, but she wasn't going to attempt to explain to Mary Hardrup what the house meant to her.

'Vicky Kelvedon's selling her house,' Mary Hardrup said.

'I hadn't heard,' Robin said. 'I thought she was with her mother in Surrey.'

'She's been in a private loony bin,' Mary Hardrup went on. '*Drying out.*'

'You don't surprise me. She was hitting the bottle heavily even before the divorce.'

Mary Hardrup smiled brightly. 'You were neighbours, weren't you?' There was nothing in the words to which Robin could take exception: but everyone there had been reminded that once Vicky Kelvedon had been Clive's mistress.

'I was rather sorry for her,' Robin said. 'Bruce was never really kind to her.'

'She led him a dance,' Linda broke in. 'Never bothered to keep her fancy men out of sight either.'

'I never particularly noticed,' Robin said, 'I always got on rather well with her.'

'You have a kind nature, Robin dear,' Linda said. 'You'll say nothing about anyone, if you can't say something good.'

Robin laughed. 'Maybe I just don't care. I can't really cope with the way things are now.'

'It was better during the War,' June Thomas broke in unexpectedly, her round face flushed. 'People weren't so spoiled, they had a sense of purpose.'

'Gerry had a sense of purpose all right,' Fiona Sindram said. 'He tried to screw every girl in the West Riding. His line was that it was a patriotic duty – at dawn he was going out in his Spitfire to joust with death.'

June Thomas looked shocked. 'He got the DFC, Fiona.'

'Yes,' Fiona said, 'but what did the F stand for?'

They all burst out laughing except for June Thomas and her sister. 'I know he's behaved badly to you, Fiona, but he was a very brave man,' June Thomas said. 'We were all *proud* of him.' Gerry Sindram was related to her as many people in Hailton were.

'All right, then,' Fiona said. 'He served his country. But frankly I think it was a toss-up whether sexual exhaustion or the Germans were going to get him first. The War ended in the nick of time for him.'

They all laughed again, even June Thomas and Molly Villendam faintly smiling. But Robin reflected, Fiona was already painting herself into a corner, preparing herself for the role of the dashing divorcée who didn't give a damn, whose husband in the grip of the male menopause had thrown away a pearl of great price. The women she met at coffee mornings would laugh, and they'd all be girls together and let their hair down and she'd be invited to lots of other coffee mornings and maybe all-girls-together informal lunches and afternoon teas, but she wouldn't get the invitations which really counted, she wouldn't meet men socially any more. There were a lot of lonely evenings and lonely weekends ahead for Fiona.

The conversation was taken over again by Mary Hardrup, who seemed positively febrile in her desire to pass on all the scandal of the neighbourhood. It was as if it were an oppression to her until she told it, as if she really did have to get it off her chest or die. Robin took it all in and made the correct replies in the correct tone – which was one of lively interest but of course firm condemnation, for there had to be decent standards. She knew that at a coffee morning somewhere else Mary Hardrup would be spilling the beans about her, Robin, that those restless eyes had been watching her expression when she mentioned Vicky Kelvedon. She and Tower House would live through it and the measurements for the new loose covers in a pattern and colours quite different from the present ones had already been taken and . . . after much thought, she'd decided to redecorate the morning-room. She would look after Tower House and it would look after her. And in the meantime the house was happy, fulfilling its *raison d'être* of accommodating people with no strain, of providing much more than shelter: it was doing its job as happily, indeed, as a sheepdog herding sheep or a retriever bringing back a gamebird to its master. Tower House actually needed people and needed a harmonious routine. What it didn't need, what it vehemently rejected, was change, the harsh voice, the raw emotion. It wasn't one of the stately homes of England, it wasn't crammed with art treasures, if ever she had to give it up it wouldn't shatter her life, but it was her home and her refuge and the arrangements she'd made over a year ago all worked. She darted a glance at Fiona, who was now moodily smoking, no longer the centre of attention, and reflected that already Gerry was being built up into a sex athlete, a roaring boy the women couldn't keep their hands off: not so long ago it had been a different story, he'd been all talk and wham-bam-thank-you-Mam: another year and it would be different again, he would in retrospect have become to Fiona the perfect husband, seduced almost against his will, the helpless victim of an unscrupulous teenage tart. And still she would have lonely evenings and lonely weekends. It wasn't fair: but that's the way it was.

By noon as if in response to a signal, the guests began to leave and Joan had come in to clear away. Mary Hardrup was the last to go; as she picked up her handbag she said in an almost hectoring tone to Robin: 'Your dear brother-in-law Donald really is much better, you know.'

'I'm very glad to hear it,' Robin said. 'We're very fond of him.'

'Linda seems over the moon,' Mary Hardrup said. She looked intently at Robin as if measuring the effect of her words.

'She has been worried about his health for a long time,' Robin said. 'It must be a relief that the new treatment is working.'

'Whatever it may be,' Mary Hardrup said. 'Whatever it may be . . . It's been lovely to see you, dear Robin.' There was a swift peck on Robin's cheek and she was gone.

'I wonder what that was about?' Robin said, half to herself.

'Nothing to gladden your heart, you may be sure Mrs Lendrick,' Joan said, stacking the coffee cups.

'She doesn't look very well herself lately,' Robin said.

'She's every right not to look very well,' Joan said. Her voice deepened. 'A year from now Mrs Hardrup'll not be here. Or if she is, she'll wish she wasn't. What she's got can't be cured at the chemist's.'

'She hasn't said anything.'

'I dare say she hasn't been told. She'll find out. All I know is that she's seen the specialist from Leeds – Mr Rillerton – funny little chap he is, but very clever.'

'You're better informed than me,' Robin said.

'Well, you know how folk talk,' Joan said. She touched the silver coffee-pot caressingly. 'Lovely piece, that . . . They don't make them like that any more . . . It's her womb. Mind, it might be something and nothing.'

'It won't be nothing,' Robin said. A gust of rain pattered against the window and the sky darkened.

'It's as well none of us knows what's in store for us,' Joan said with dismal relish.

'Nice things sometimes happen,' Robin said brightly.

'I wouldn't count on it, Mrs Lendrick. I wouldn't count on it.'

Resting after lunch – a boiled egg, toast and coffee – in the morning-room on her new chaise-longue from Heals, she was glad of the mohair rug over her. It wasn't a cold house and the morning-room was the warmest room in it. But the rug was a comfort, like a child's security blanket. She wasn't thinking of Mary Hardrup, who was far from being an intimate friend. Mary was simply someone who'd been around a long time, with whom she had gone to school, whose home she had visited – but not a real friend, not a sharing friend. But she was someone who Robin needed, as well she might need Robin; she fitted into the pattern of life like the river or the railway station or the Town Hall or the parish church. Of course she didn't want her to suffer but, more important than that, she didn't want her to go away. Or, rather, to be taken away: half-asleep now, she felt that she was surely entitled to feel that she and Mary Hardrup and everyone else she knew in Hailton were there because they'd chosen to be and living as they chose to live: Mary Hardrup wouldn't have chosen cancer.

Robin was overcome by sleep and awoke at half-past five to a now rather too stuffy room and with the beginnings of a headache. But Mary Hardrup had been dismissed from her mind, and after a shower and a change into a new dress just for the hell of it – it was longer than mini but shorter than the length she usually wore – she brewed herself tea and took the tray into the study. A shower was drumming on the windows and the sky outside had darkened. She found a line from a play taking over: *The wind and the rain in your face, Gribaud, the wind and the rain in your face* . . . She repeated the words to herself softly: she had reached a point of stillness and was content to be alone. Alone but not lonely, though she had the house to herself: Clive, it being Wednesday, wouldn't be back until late, and Petronella was going on a theatre trip straight from school. But Petronella would be home later and they'd talk about the show and have a little supper together; Clive would be home later than Petronella and they wouldn't talk about where he'd been but there'd be goodwill between them and an implicit understanding that they wouldn't rock the boat: and the household would continue and she and Clive would entertain and be entertained, there'd be a purposeful shape to their lives, there'd be a satisfying routine. She'd finished her tea and taken up a piece of embroidery when the front doorbell rang.

When she opened the door she saw Stephen. He didn't smile at her: he stood there in silence for what seemed a long time, perfectly still, his hands clasped behind his back. He was at ease but not arrogant. She let him in without a word and took him into the study without a word. He hadn't changed since last she saw him; but then, she thought, she wouldn't have expected him to.

She sat down and he took the armchair opposite her. 'I'm tired,' he said. 'But I'm confident that I've royally screwed Deira TV.' He grinned at her.

'I told you not to come,' she said. 'I don't want to see you again.' She couldn't put any conviction into the words.

'A very wise decision. There's no future in it for you and me. There never has been. Let's face it, I'm a rotten sod. I shan't change.' He was smiling; with pain and yet with joy she realized that it was as if he were boasting.

'I faced that long ago. I don't think that I've ever met anyone as selfish as you, Stephen.' She tried not to look at him.

He lit a cheroot and stretched out his legs. 'No, you won't have. If anything, I've grown more selfish recently. Not that being Mr Nice would help me in my present job.'

'I did mean what I said on the phone. Do you want to mess up my whole life? And Jean's? And your son's?'

'You've forgotten Clive,' he said. 'He's a decent man. We really did hurt him.' His tone wasn't in the least mocking.

127

'Yes, we did hurt him. And that heart attack nearly killed him – '

'He's a decent man. I've never denied it.' He looked at her searchingly, then got up and circled the room. 'My God, you have even more stuff here than we have in dear old Weybridge. But your taste is superior to Jean's.' He ran his finger over the top of the desk. 'You really do have a home.' He sat down again. 'We have a house in which we're camping out.'

'You really don't care, do you, Stephen? You're not really listening to me. I don't think that you ever have.'

'I'm very good at listening. I've been listening off and on for nearly four hours this very day.' He smiled at her for the first time. 'And when I spoke, I simply regurgitated what they'd said. Selectively, of course. With a few amendments.'

'I'm not really interested.'

'You should be. The art of negotiation is to tell the other party what they want to hear, which is their own words, edited, of course.' He paused and looked around, as if expecting to see figures emerging from behind the furniture. 'Where's everybody?'

'Clive won't be in until late. Nor Petronella.' Her face had flushed. 'I want you to go away. You're nothing but trouble. You spoil everything – ' She stood up. 'There isn't any peace where you are. People build things – ' She stopped, fighting back the tears – 'They build things and they're beautiful, and you come in like the tide – ' She sat down again, her hands to her face, and began to sob.

He came over to her chair and knelt beside her. 'You're too big for sandcastles,' he said gently. He pulled up her skirt and kissed the bare flesh above the stocking-top. There was something reverential about the kiss, as if her naked flesh were a reliquary or a cardinal's ring. She sighed and her hands came down to his head and stroked his hair. Her eyes were still glistening with tears but now she was perfectly calm. For now he had touched her and the stillness would continue and she'd feel the wind and the rain on her face.

Ten

Two weeks after at the Hailton Players Club Night Robin at last became fully aware of what had happened. She hadn't, of course, told anyone about it, least of all Clive. And until two weeks after she had, in fact, kept the memory of that evening – four hours precisely – well to the back of her mind. The experience hadn't really belonged to her or to Stephen: it had dropped in casually, and they both had been there. Only when it chose to would it come again.

The two weeks after Stephen's return to Surrey had in any case been full ones. She and Clive had given a rather boring and tiring American customer and his wife dinner at Tower House, they'd dined out at Seth Lensholt's, they'd dined out at her sister Jennifer's in Harrogate, there'd been an exhausting meeting of the Hailton Players Management Committee and an equally exhausting meeting of the Hailton Civic Society. And last Sunday they'd had people – far too many people – in for drinks in the morning and it had gone on until past three and got a little rowdy, though she and Clive had been able to handle it and Joan had been able to remove the stain on the study carpet, though grumbling about it in an objectionably puritanical and this-isn't-really-my-job kind of way. And on Monday when she'd been looking forward to a quiet evening and supper on a tray, Clive had brought a customer from Frankfurt in to take pot luck, but she'd seen at a glance that pot luck as far as this customer was concerned wasn't going to mean poached egg on toast or fish and chips or cottage pie.

She'd survived it all and had done her job and wasn't complaining; she'd known what she was taking on when she'd married Clive some twenty-three years ago. But now, sipping Scotch on the rocks at the Atlanta Hall in the street next to the theatre, she was grateful that Clive had gone away to London that morning and wouldn't be back until late Friday. She'd survived the fortnight and so had Clive; and now she was sitting with Malcolm Fareland and Norman, listening to them bickering about the New Wave in the theatre without any particular interest but making the right noises from time to time. Malcolm was a tall, thin young man given to sudden explosive enthusiasms which always seemed to take him completely by surprise. He was an articled clerk in his father's office and his father, Walter Fareland, Clive's lawyer, had said more than once that he might go far if only he didn't confuse law with justice. He was appealing to Robin for support now. 'Robin, darling, can't you see that the stage has got to open out? To reject the picture frame?'

'I like the picture frame,' she said. 'So do John Osborne and Joe Orton.'

Norman snorted. 'Osborne and Orton? Darling, what on earth does that prove? Osborne and Orton just give a new twist to the dear old well-made play – '

And she let it go over her head and simply smiled: neither of them much cared what she thought anyway. She was here and at home amongst the people she knew, had in some instances known all her life, and still the golden and purple flock wallpaper induced an atmosphere of opulent cosiness, still the Windsor chairs painted in different colours added light-heartedness to the cosiness. The Atlanta Hall – no one ever called it the Players' Hall and the Management Committee had given up trying – was a separate building from the theatre and yet it belonged to the theatre. It wasn't a public hall, it wasn't a commercial enterprise: it was like a club and yet much more than a club.

And outside was Hailton High Street, which even under the harsh blue-green glare of the new sodium lights always extended a warm welcome, always seemed a street on which

130

one could stand and gossip, a street along which one could stroll. The buildings were unremarkable, but predominantely Victorian and in local stone. There'd been sporadic redevelopment in the 1930s but the new buildings – including the Atlanta Hall itself in red brick and single-storied, next to the main council car park – all fitted in. The High Street was unplanned and haphazard but sustainingly harmonious, an unexpectedly tasty scratch meal. Perhaps it wouldn't be like this much longer: a new supermarket and a new office block were coming and old-established shops which were part of her childhood all seemed to have gone out of business. And the small streets north and south of the High Street were being demolished almost daily; there were more and more stretches of rubble-strewn desolation.

But still she had this feeling about the High Street and still she felt that the High Street returned the feeling, and still there were the dark waters of the river, and still she was in her own particular place. She took out the memory of the four hours with Stephen, handling it very carefully. It had nothing to do with what she felt now; she liked her own world more and more and Stephen's world less and less. The people in her world were far from being soft. But they stayed around. When someone came to the end of his credit and his cheques bounced and his children were taken away from their private schools and the Building Society foreclosed the mortgage and the vultures of the Inland Revenue swooped, some sort of job would always be found for him. There'd be somewhere for him to live, he'd still exist as a person: people would still acknowledge his existence and pass the time of day with him. If you fell, you were allowed to pick yourself up and walk on, though moving more slowly. In Stephen's world, when you fell you were trodden down. They just didn't see you if you weren't on your feet and keeping pace with the rest.

These thoughts were always evoked by Stephen but now, after what had happened within five minutes of him having touched her, in her bedroom without preamble, without even taking off her dress, they had no more to do with concepts like right or wrong or good or bad than had the points of the compass or the state of the weather. It had been like the first time on the night of Clive's forty-seventh birthday party, in that very room, on that very bed. And it had been equally as quick and savage, but this time her pleasure was his and his pleasure hers, and he'd stayed inside her; they'd been absolutely one flesh. That had been the best of all.

Norman pinched her arm. 'You haven't been listening, dear heart.'

'She hasn't been agreeing with your every word,' Malcolm said.

'She's been on automatic pilot,' Norman said peevishly. 'It's a trick of hers, my dear Malcolm. She goes on with her own life whilst graciously acknowledging the presence of her inferiors. Like royalty riding by in the golden state coach, smiling from side to side and giving tight little waves . . . ' he mimicked the expression and the gesture. 'You don't suppose that royalty's really thinking *what nice people*! You don't suppose that royalty's thinking about the people at all, do you?' Now there was real hostility in his voice.

'Take it easy,' she said. 'I was woolgathering. Don't you ever woolgather?'

He scowled at her, his whole body tensed as if he were about to attack her physically, then almost collapsed, seeming as if shrinking and becoming older. 'I told you, Robin, I hide in a corner of the hayfield from the men with guns.' He got up. 'Excuse me.'

Malcolm looked embarrassed: as embarrassed as if he himself had actually committed some *faux pas*. 'I'm sorry, Robin. Really, I don't know what he's going on about – '

She patted his hand. 'It wasn't you,' she said. 'Norman can be very touchy. Don't pay any attention.' She rose unhurriedly. 'See you later.' She wouldn't see him later if she could help it: he was too young, too naïve, too earnest, in fact rather a bore, but she didn't want either to be stuck with him talking about the New Wave or have him leave her first, on her own as if no one wanted her. It was one of the things her mother had taught her: always leave first, never be left alone. And let them come to you.

At the table near the bar she saw her brother-in-law Donald; he beckoned her over with an almost imperious gesture. 'Come and join us, Robin love.' He looked healthier and in better spirits than she'd ever seen him: his face was rosier, even his thinning hair – darker than Clive's – seemed thicker and more lustrous. He waved at the bottle of hock. 'I'll get you a glass.'

'Not just now, thank you,' she said, sitting down. 'I'm going soon, anyway.'

Donald refilled his glass. 'A little wine for the stomach's sake,' he said, not drunkenly but rather owlishly. 'Do you good, Robin. You're looking a bit peaked.'

Linda rapped his hand sharply. 'Donald, you never say things like that to a lady!' But there was no real reproof in her voice. 'Robin looks absolutely marvellous as always.' The tone of the remark was perfunctory.

Robin smiled, widening her eyes. 'Donald's right, Linda. It's been a tiring week. It's me for an early night and a mug of Ovaltine.'

'Ah, pooh to that!' Linda said, holding her glass out to Donald. 'One can get in an absolute rut. I'm so tired of nights in slippers by the telly. Mind, it's such a business getting baby-sitters. And they want to be paid these days – '

'It's not our problem any more,' Robin said.

'They grow up so quickly,' Linda said. She sighed theatrically. 'It won't be long before there's just us two old things, will it, Donald?'

'You'll never be old to me, my love.' He blew a kiss to her and to Robin's surprise lit a cheroot.

Robin arched her eyebrows. Donald laughed. She hadn't heard him laugh very often in all the years she'd known him, but when she had it had been a creaky, harsh, almost painful laugh. His laugh now was easy and full-throated. 'Only gave them up because of the old tum,' he said. 'Now I'm back in the human race.' He blew out smoke noisily. 'I'm going to be a devil tonight and have cheese and pickled onions for supper.'

'I'm happy you're so much better,' Robin said.

'It's this new drug,' Linda said. 'More than an antacid, really . . . He's a new man.'

'I can see,' Robin said. But she wasn't quite sure she liked the new Donald: the old Donald had been a fusspot and a moaner, frightened of his own shadow, but she'd always found that there was something rather endearing about him, he was a struggler and a castaway, aware of his imperfections. The new Donald was too pleased with himself by half.

'A lot of new faces here tonight,' Linda commented, taking in the room in one swift glance. 'I don't seem to know anyone.'

'I hadn't noticed,' Robin said. She was remembering Stephen again now, remembering driving away from Tower House with him in the Jaguar and not giving a damn what the neighbours thought.

'I notice Norman's here,' Linda said. 'He was never away from the place once and then he seemed to turn off it.'

Robin smiled faintly. 'I suppose he found other interests.'

'Can't make chaps like him out,' Donald said. 'He still lives with his partner, doesn't he? Ruth Inglewood?'

'So I hear,' Robin said, mildly irritated. Donald would not be quite as interested in the Ruth-Norman *ménage* as Linda, but he knew very well what the situation was. She detached herself from it, back again with Stephen in her bedroom in Tower House. She had been astonished then that so hasty and greedy a coupling could bring such complete and wordless fulfilment: she was not astonished now but simply content to remember it. It seemed to her that whatever she'd had before belonged in the past to someone else, that she was, so to speak, in a snug and well-ordered bourgeois commune; but what she had with Stephen was hers and hers alone.

134

'Doesn't Norman go around with that young man from the gift shop?' Linda asked her.

'Gary? I've heard something to that effect.' She kept her voice toneless. There had been a time, just after Clive had recovered from his heart attack when she and Clive and Ruth had come to an understanding, it had really been a question of justice, and least said soonest mended, of no one being hurt. And then Norman had somehow crept in, become intimate with them. He didn't take any liberties, he didn't ask for anything, but he became too chummy, he'd confide to her and Clive secrets they didn't want to know and would expect in return from them secrets they didn't want to give away. They wouldn't have been very big or terrible secrets; but for their marriage to continue and for the understanding to continue, those secrets had to be kept.

'Everybody has their own idea of pleasure.' Donald put his hand over Linda's and smiled at her fondly. He really did seem to be riding high, Robin thought; and Linda, though she'd never be anything else but plain and her dress sense never anything else than disastrous, seemed as if she'd shed twenty years.

'Clive's back from London on Saturday, isn't he?' Linda asked. 'We're having a little party in the evening. We'd love to have you.' She paused as if to emphasize the chief inducement. 'Bruce and Tracy will be there.'

'I'm sure Clive will be delighted if he's not too tired. He has to take it easy – '

'Ah, naturally. None of us is getting any younger. The time's come for him to ease up a bit . . . '

'Oh, he's still far from being ancient,' said Robin lightly. 'A shower and a rest and a drink and he'll be the life and soul of the party.' And again she asked herself the question: why are they both so triumphant, why do they both so obviously see themselves as top dogs?

'Selling is tougher and tougher these days,' Donald said. 'Clive's really where the action is. Business is total war, not a

135

cricket match at Headingley.' He assumed a stern expression, addressing his troops.

'Clive doesn't have any illusions,' she said primly. 'Not when dealing with the French. He doesn't even like them. He says they've let us down in two wars.'

'I hope that he doesn't tell them that,' Donald said.

'He probably will,' Robin said flippantly. 'Just for a laugh.'

Donald perceptibly winced. 'They're terribly touchy,' he said. For a moment he was the old Donald, the harried and going round in circles and sure that he'd carry the can. But his face cleared quickly. 'You're joking,' he said.

'Of course, Donald. I'm sure he'll come back with a sheaf of orders.' She yawned. 'Excuse me, I'd rather like an early night for once.'

'It's a big house for one person,' Linda said. 'Don't you ever feel lonely?'

'There's Petronella. She's having friends in. The hi-fi will be belting it out full blast.' She stood up. 'I'll be seeing you.'

'Saturday at eight,' Linda said. 'If Clive's got over the journey.'

'He's very resilient,' Robin said. 'More than you'd imagine.' And as she kissed them and went out she was remembering Stephen again, remembering his stubby capable fingers, his somehow incongruous manicure, and his rather bad-tempered face with its five o'clock shadow. Even if the hi-fi was going full blast when she got home, she wouldn't hear it, she'd hear only that harsh voice which never said anything with the intention of pleasing her, which mocked her, mocked himself, mocked the whole of life: he wasn't querulous or self-pitying, but he wouldn't ever be satisfied. But after the act of love he had, after all, stayed inside her and he'd held her and there had been kindness and tenderness, a special sort of kindness and tenderness, delicate flowers growing from the jagged granite. And driving away from Tower House he'd said something which had surprised her, which wasn't in character. 'You make me wish to be different,' he'd said. 'I don't know exactly how.'

'I don't want to change you,' she'd said. 'I've never tried to.'

'It's bloody ridiculous,' he'd said. 'What the hell are we doing here? I'll fuck things up for you, I know I will – ' They had been then on the narrow road leading to the Cow and Calf rocks, with drystone walls on the right and the open moors rising to the left, and it was already growing dark.

'You did that, two years ago. I got over it.' Her hand had stroked his thigh and she had found that she could hardly breathe; what her hand was doing had been responsible for that, but she'd known that what would follow, with any sort of luck, would enable her to breathe again.

'I think we ought to stop,' he'd said, and turned off the road on the track leading to the level patch of ground hard by the Calf, the big smooth level-topped rock pitted with footholds, which was hard by the cliffs of the Cow. A child could climb up the Calf from the side nearest the Cow, and there was a panoramic view of the valley – mostly arable and urban, very civilized – from the flat top. And the rain had stopped and the sun was going down, but this was now limestone country and the rocks would hold the light.

'It's some time since I've been here,' she had said when he'd brought the car to a sudden stop. 'Daddy brought us here a lot when we were little.' And she'd let her hand rest and unexpectedly found herself breathing more easily.

He'd lit a cheroot and had wound the window down. It had been very warm inside the car and she'd been grateful for the fresh rain-washed air. 'How is Clive?' he'd asked.

'I'm not really thinking about him,' she'd said. 'Why should you?'

'Godammit, I can't help it! I don't mean I'm feeling guilty, but I bloody well am.' He'd looked puzzled and not quite himself. 'I feel so bloody *odd*! Lost, bloody well lost . . . But I do feel happy.' He'd put his hand on top of hers. 'I'm not pleased with myself, though, I don't like that.'

'I didn't ask you to come,' she'd said. Again she'd found it hard to breathe: and had started to stroke his thigh again and had seen in the half-light his lips draw back over his teeth as if in pain.

All this was in her mind in every detail as she walked out of the Atlanta Hall; none of it showed on her face. She was smiling very faintly, but it was a long-practised smile, proclaiming goodwill and friendliness but also making it plain that she hadn't time to stop, she really was going home. But the home that those who saw her assumed she was going to wasn't the home she was actually going to. Her home to them was a home like their own, an actual dwell.ng needing to be maintained, with rates charged by the Hailton Urban District Council. Her home to herself was a place to dream in, was whatever she chose to make it – an enchanted castle or in an enchanted kingdom, a place where there were no limits, where the water of everyday existence was changed into wine.

And of all the people at the Atlanta Hall that evening few would have understood this. Even Donald and Linda, though they understood about love, couldn't have put themselves into her shoes. Norman could have done, with only a small effort; but Norman was only there that evening because things were beginning to hurt. Things weren't hurting for Robin, and as she walked out of the Atlanta Hall towards her car she honestly didn't believe that they ever would.

Eleven

It was drizzling when Robin got into the car, but even then she'd have liked the top down: the air smelled fresh and clean after the smoky atmosphere which she had just left. She'd enjoyed her evening, but being alone was what mattered now. It was very quiet as it always was in Hailton at this time; but there were a few lights on in the buildings around the car park. Hailton wasn't absolutely dead, because a few people still lived in the town centre: there was no life in the street but life was going on somewhere.

The river was east of the High Street, out of sight now behind the two blocks of old terraced houses which bordered the car park to the left. The cobbled alley between the two blocks of houses would take her through a small courtyard and then through another cobbled alley to the footpath by the river. She reflected as she unlocked her car that it was a long time since she had walked by the river and that she'd never walked there with Stephen and it wasn't likely that she ever would. But what she suddenly wanted now was to walk alone, on that narrow path beside the dark waters, with the dark woods rising on the other side. Dark waters and dark woods, she thought: what else would they be at this hour but dark?

She got into the car and sat still for a moment, summoning up Stephen's face. Sometimes for no good reason she couldn't see it with any precision, couldn't determine even whether it was dark or swarthy, saturnine or on the verge of a sneer. His features were actually quite good – bold, decisive, aggressive, in proportion – and his grey eyes intelligent, but somehow they were as if thrown together in a hurry. He didn't have a patient face, he didn't have a kind face. But it suited her, just as his ferociously compact body suited her. She wasn't ever really comfortable with him as still she was comfortable with Clive, but for the time being comfort wasn't what she wanted.

She knew very well that she wouldn't walk by the river: but she did long for it keenly for a moment, she did want to push everything and everybody away so as to be nearer to Stephen. To be nearer didn't mean conversation: a fortnight ago they'd had that, and had it in full measure. For all their words had had an extra dimension. They were heavy words – not dull or ponderous or slow-moving, but terrible in their power.

Yes, the point is reiterated: she was a romantic. There on the large patch of levelled-off wasteland which was the Council car park she was being taken out of herself. She wasn't asking herself *Is this all?* Instead, two weeks after, she was exclaiming in surprise *I didn't know there'd be so much.* She was overwhelmed and awe-struck by what she'd been given, irrespective of the fact that what had been in Stephen's mind in the first place must only have been to take. It had all been so unceremonious and unadorned and urgent, without even the dignity of nakedness, but no matter how often and how long she looked at it there'd been nothing better in all her experience. And they'd meet again and it would be even better, the commonplace would be abolished and life would irresistibly ascend.

Her mood was actually a mood of yearning, and even the fact that her car was a Triumph Vitesse helped this mood along. It wasn't a big car, but it had a lively six-cylinder engine, a high power-to-weight ratio and responsive steering. Robin cared very little about cars and had only barely noted that Stephen's Jaguar in 1969 was appreciably bigger, more powerful and more luxuriously appointed than the Jaguar he'd had in 1967. Nevertheless she now somehow did appreciate that the Triumph was the proper car for a heroine of high romance.

She got into the car and turned on the ignition: it started at once, and she switched on the radio and pushed in the button to send up the aerial. She somehow never expected this to work and was always almost childishly delighted when it did. As usual, it was a Beatles song – 'All you need is love' – but she didn't try for another channel because, for once, that was what she felt. There were times when the Beatles said nothing to her that she wanted to hear, when they used an argot which she felt described cruelty and madness and despair, but this song was both potent and wholesome and when she came to think of it, not cheap. In this, like Norman, she'd have preferred something from Noël Coward, Sigmund Romberg, or even Ivor Novello, but it would take her home, it would carry her through, it would maintain the proper rhythm, it would both soothe and stimulate.

And now she was stimulated, driving much faster than usual, taking chances she wouldn't normally have taken and could only take because she knew the road so well. She came into the double bend half a mile before Throstlehill village at fifty, knowing very well that thirty was the maximum approach speed, and came out of it on the wrong side of the road with the brakes screeching and the tyres on the verge of a skid, aware that there was a thirty-foot drop beyond the wall, aware that three cars had gone through that wall in the last four years, aware and not caring, still only with Stephen. She didn't have the death wish: but at the second she went into the corner she was giving concrete shape to an ever-growing feeling that death, like the evening at the Atlanta, like the dark river and the dark wood, like the quietness and the secret corners of Hailton, was part of a whole. She hadn't been frightened and, at the second the skid began she'd taken her foot off the brake and the Triumph had taken itself out of trouble, seeming to move as delicately as a cat. She had actually been very lucky; if she'd delayed taking her foot off the brake a fraction of a second longer, if there'd been anything coming the other way, there'd have been another gap in the wall and another wrecked car with a mangled corpse within it in the stony field thirty feet below. The last victim of the bend, a handsome and cheerful woman who'd been Miss Hailton of 1948, had actually ended up mangled but not a corpse, and though her artificial leg wasn't apparent under slacks and she'd learned to use it by heroic effort, there was nothing much that could be done to make her face recognizable as human. One way and another she had a lot of pain, too.

Robin knew all this but regained the left-hand side of the road with her pulse unquickened and slowed down only when leaving the road for the village green. There was a half-smile on her face of which she was wholly unconscious. Lights were still on in the houses around the village green and there was the sound of music from the village hall. She didn't think in terms of a narrow escape from death, much less congratulate herself on her skilful driving. But as she drove down Chipfield Close she had somehow a sense of triumph. When she got out of the car the rain had stopped. She was quite calm now, but Stephen was still with her. She was still ascending and the rain had brought out the smell of the pinewoods which sheltered the village.

There was a blast of sound from Petronella's room as she entered Tower House and nearly every light in the house seemed to be on. She found Petronella in the kitchen drinking tea. She was in her pyjamas and a blue towelling dressing-gown: she looked thin and young and defenceless. Robin kissed her. 'All your friends gone?'

'I've a test tomorrow,' Petronella rubbed her eyes. 'The tea's just made.'

Robin got herself a mug from the Welsh dresser and sat down. 'Did anybody ring?'

'Daddy rang. He says he has a chance of outwitting the bloody Frogs. And not to forget to stir up the plumber.'

Robin drank her tea. For once Petronella had got it right, not too weak and just strong enough to be slightly astringent, to give her a lift. 'I'm working on it, but he's never in.' The kitchen was warm and clean and tidy but not too tidy: this was a home, but she'd have liked more people in it, would almost have wished Petronella's friends to have stayed and cooked themselves a snack; the kitchen needed the smell of warm food. She took one of Petronella's Gauloises.

'I thought you'd given up,' Petronella said.

'I like one occasionally.'

'Everybody goes on about it so damned much, it makes you want it all the more.'

'I know the feeling,' Robin said. 'There's always something that's bad for you.' She and Petronella were exchanging goodwill and recognition signals now: no more, no less. That was fine – mother and daughter having a hot drink at bedtime, Daddy out in the cold wilderness hunting game for supper, the reassuring routine going on.

'They go on alarmingly about it at St Perpetua's,' Petronella said, yawning. 'That and drinking . . . Oh, I forgot – someone rang from a call-box. Said it was a wrong number.' Her dark eyes were suddenly hard.

'Well, I expect that's what it was,' Robin said lightly. Again and not at the same level, different in degree but not in kind, there was the feeling she had just before the Triumph's tyres took hold again. Stephen had said that he'd be in touch but hadn't been in touch; it hadn't spoiled what she'd had and what she had now and she didn't want any promises and wouldn't make any promises herself. She was tired of promises, tired of being bound, tired of being a pillar of society: she wanted to play it by ear. But, of course, it wasn't a wrong number and Petronella had latched on to it.

Petronella's eyes dropped. 'I suppose so,' she said. She lit another cigarette. 'Mummy, I think if I go to Charbury, I'll go into a Hall of Residence.'

'You don't know whether you'll get a place yet,' Robin said. 'I really wouldn't recommend living in Charbury anyway. It's getting very rough.'

'Why shouldn't I live in a rough place?' Petronella asked. 'Other people have to. What's so special about me?'

143

'Yes, but *you* don't have to.' She recognized wearily that Petronella was about to start an argument. She put aside Stephen's face, the picture of him driving out to a phone box simply to hear her voice: he needed her, as much as she needed him. 'But what difference does it make what *I* think?'

'There isn't anything you care about!' Petronella burst out. 'You and Daddy – all your friends – you're sleepwalkers. You don't want to change anything, you don't want to make anything better – '

Robin sighed. 'All right, darling, all right. Why so fierce? I don't really give a damn about anything else except getting on with my own life. Neither does your father.'

'No. You're not telling lies. That's why you look so damned young. Too young.'

'I'm sorry. I'll try to acquire a few more wrinkles . . . ' She smiled. 'And stop wearing a bra and girdle.'

'You're not like Olive's mother. Or Auntie Linda.' Petronella's voice was accusing.

Robin shrugged. 'And your father isn't like Leo Villendam. Or your Uncle Donald either. What are we supposed to do about it?' Stephen wasn't there any more, now she – and Clive too – were under judgement. She wasn't quite certain of her crime and she didn't accept the authority of her judge; but now it occurred to her, and not for the first time, that when she was Petronella's age her parents were middle-aged and they must have begun to be middle-aged, to accept the role of father and mother soon after the birth of her younger sister. There would have been a brief period when they were a young mother and a young father, endearingly comic figures worried out of their minds, raw recruits doing their best, supported by the whole of society. It wasn't the same now. There wasn't any support.

'I don't know what you're supposed to do! How should I know?' Petronella's tone appealed for help and yet was aggressive. 'But why do you hang on to this great big house, for a start? It's spooky. Really spooky.'

'Why should you care?' Robin asked coldly. 'You're not going to be here, are you?'

'It wasn't always like this,' Petronella said. She was now looking at Robin as if from a great distance. 'You and Daddy were more – well, *here*. It feels more like a hotel now.'

'I'm here most of the time,' Robin said. 'If Daddy isn't here it's because of business. What on earth do you want?'

Petronella looked down at her mug of tea as if expecting to find the answer there. She looked at Robin again, this time as a child seeking reassurance. Robin would have given her that reassurance, but wasn't sure how to give it to her . . .

'I do love you, dear,' she said gently, and put her hand on Petronella's.

'I know,' Petronella said and stood up. 'I'm going to bed. Good night.' She kissed Robin on the forehead and walked out of the kitchen slowly. If she had been a child, then Robin's response to that defeated droop of the shoulders and those dragging feet would have been to gather her into her arms. And she'd have cried and what was bothering her would have all come out, she'd have let herself go, and large warm strong Mummy would have held her tight and taken her up to bed and tucked her up with her teddy bear. And she would have slid smoothly and happily into sleep, happily and willingly with the nightlight burning and the rain tapping gently at the window. If she'd awakened in the small hours and been frightened of the nightlight going out, if the rain had been tapping too insistently – bony fingers of something wanting to be let in – she would have crawled into bed between Clive and Robin and settled down snugly between them, a small warm totally trusting animal now completely secure.

But she was nearly eighteen now, searching for her identity, needing desperately to do her own thing when she had found out what her own thing was, and Mummy was one of the decadent bourgeoisie, someone to be always argued with. But she wasn't Mummy any more. Robin said to herself: she was a figure of high romance, she was steering into the skid, she was supremely herself and had paid her biological dues. She knew what her own thing was and she was doing it, and Stephen had phoned. She'd hear from him again as he'd hear from her: pride didn't matter any more. It was fine for him to pursue her, but she'd pursue him if necessary. Tower House had been their place and the back seat of the Jaguar had been their place; but there wasn't anywhere they wouldn't take over, exclude everyone else from, make absolutely their own.

She sat quite still, her hands now on the table as if at a séance. She'd stubbed out her cigarette, she wasn't drinking her tea. Her face was absolutely still. She was looking at someone else across the table. She wasn't looking at that person as if expecting any kind of action or any sort of statement. They were sharing something which had come from outside themselves, they were as if conscripted into a huge conspiracy. She sat there for a full half hour, her eyes bright. She wasn't impatient. Stephen had phoned and there'd be all the time in the world.

Twelve

When Clive had phoned Tower House from London he had indeed been certain that he had a chance of outwitting the Frogs. It wasn't really a question of outwitting them but simply of fair exchange. Lendrick Mills would buy a new French stain-proofing process and their true-and-tried French customer would continue to buy cloth from Lendrick Mills. Buy did, of course, mean buy at a price which afforded Lendrick Mills a reasonable profit: and in his own experience the French were far worse than the Dutch. They did worse than give you too little: they wanted to give you nothing at all. But just for once the French had been as rational and logical as they claimed to be, and when he'd got back home on Friday, it had seemed to him just a matter of getting the paperwork right. It wasn't that he'd done anything illegal or in any way questionable, but that the essential deal couldn't be done on paper: it was all person-to-person. And it had all been over bar the shouting on Friday, and he'd explained it all to Donald and had forgotten and relaxed over the weekend and then found himself lunching with Seth Lensholt and Diana Keysham at Ferrand's Chophouse in Charbury on Thursday the following week with· Donald becoming increasingly obstructive and elusive and no one from the true-and-tried French customer ever having phoned.

He would like to have explained this to Seth and Diana but didn't really know how to. Seth was a shareholder and a director and Diana was a shareholder determined to be a director, but on the Thursday of the week following his negotiations with the true-and-tried French customer in London he quite honestly didn't care.

147

Ferrand's Chophouse was an old-established restaurant hard by the Wool Exchange. It was small, red-carpeted, oak-panelled, with blue plush banquettes and the best steaks and Barnsley chops in the West Riding, and a surprisingly good range of wines. Clive generally enjoyed eating there; today he would have settled for a sandwich and a glass of milk.

'Don't you like your steak?' Seth Lensholt asked.

'It's fine,' Clive said. He nibbled a roll. 'I'm just not terribly hungry.'

Seth chewed noisily. 'You want to watch it,' he said. 'Wouldn't suit you being thin. Good meat never did anyone any harm.'

Clive sipped his wine. It was soft yet robust, just what he liked and not too damned warm either, but suddenly it made him think of blood. He put it down.

'Look, Seth, just what are you and Diana trying to drive at? About this French deal?'

Seth's square dour face attempted to be placatory but failed, the tight mouth grinning but the eyes menacing. 'No need to stir yourself up, lad. We just feel you've taken a bit too much on.'

'Frankly, we don't trust them,' Diana Keysham said. 'And we'd like to know a great deal more about what they have to sell us.'

Clive looked at her sourly. The long blonde hair, china-blue eyes and *retroussé* nose didn't seem to him to fit in with that clipped arrogant upper-class voice. The face – and the low-cut peach silk blouse – belonged to a saucy soubrette. The voice was that of a martinet headmistress and he was the Naughtiest Girl in the Fifth. And what was she doing there anyway? She was a big shareholder but not that big.

'There's ample information available,' he said. 'As I've been reminding you for over an hour now.'

'What I and Diana – and a few other shareholders – feel is that we've been here before,' Seth said. 'It's not just a matter

148

of the deal itself. We sell the Frogs something and their civil servants work to rule. If they can make it awkward for us, they will.'

'But *our* civil servants are thoroughly decent chaps,' Diana said. 'No obstacles are placed in the way of our French friends.'

Clive took a gulp of wine. He still didn't like the taste, but he needed some kind of lift. 'Christ, do you think I didn't know that? That's the whole bloody point. Our sodding bureaucracy isn't on our side. Frog bureaucrats are on the side of Frog businessmen. That's what it's all about. Lendrick Mills buys this wonderful French stain-proofing process so the French port authorities let our cloth in. It's as simple as that.'

Seth scowled. 'Is it? I know the buggers. You can have the bloody French imprint. But if they're that way out they'll just say it's not up to standard. After we've paid for this sodding process.' He scowled again. 'Do you think we haven't any ideas about stain-proofing in Charbury?' His pale blue eyes were for a moment hurt and distracted. 'I say don't trust the buggers. I was there at Passchendaele.'

'All right, Seth,' Clive said gently. 'Tell me what you want to do. Not that I'll commit myself,' he added cautiously.

'You'd better wake up.' Seth suddenly had transformed. 'I don't like the present arrangements. And I'm not alone.'

Clive found his head beginning to throb. 'You just tell me how to deal with this particular problem.'

'Bruce Kelvedon has a few ideas on the subject,' Diana Keysham said. 'Not that you'll listen.'

'Bruce has a few ideas about computers, which mostly boil down to us installing more of the bloody things, whether we need them or not. I wasn't aware he knew much about the export trade. Or high-grade worsted, for that matter.'

'It isn't just Bruce who has ideas about the policy of Lendrick Mills,' Seth said. He pointed an accusing finger at Clive. 'You're a bit of a one-man band, aren't you, Clive lad?'

'I'm the shareholders' representative, not their delegate.'

Clive's head was hurting now. 'And I have a majority shareholding.'

'No, no. You and Donald have a majority shareholding between you. That's not the same thing.'

'It damn well is.' Clive took a deep breath. 'That's how my father intended it.' He wasn't in control, he thought; they were ganging up on him. He noticed the swell of Diana Keysham's breasts momentarily and it made him feel worse: he could have endured it better if she'd been hatchet-faced and dowdy, bulging or skeletal.

'You'll find that you're mistaken,' she said, a note of amusement in her voice.

'Has he been selling his shares?' He felt bile rising to his throat. 'He's daft enough to do it.'

'I know nowt about that. But you might find he doesn't always see eye-to-eye with you.' Seth was genuinely smiling now.

'He'll see more eye-to-eye with Bruce Kelvedon, you mean?'

Seth shrugged. 'Donald would like more say in things.'

Clive hunted in his pocket for the antacid tablets he'd recently started to use. 'I can find out if Donald's sold any shares.'

Diana Keysham looked amused. 'He needn't have actually sold any shares, need he? Because it's Tracy who's got the money. She mightn't want to lash out to that extent. But there could be a comparatively cheap way of getting Donald's – well, unstinted support.' Her face was quite serious but Clive felt she was holding her laughter back. And her laughter was also a sexual challenge.

'I know my own brother,' he said. 'And his liking for a flutter. You mean that Bruce has paid his debts – or Tracy has. And now Bruce and Tracy have him by the balls.'

Diana Keysham raised her eyebrows. 'You're being rather crude.'

'Sorry,' Clive said. 'They have his undivided attention.' He succeeded in extricating two antacid tablets from the tightly wrapped roll. 'If you'll excuse me, I've forgotten an engagement.' He stood up, the taste in his mouth growing worse. He kept the antacid tablets in his hand, feeling irrationally that if he was seen taking them he really had been defeated.

Seth's face now wore an expression of complete satisfaction. It occurred to Clive that it wasn't really a square face but rather one assembled from interlocking blocks, on the same principle as a Lego set. The present expression of rather brutal satisfaction was well within its range; friendship or any kind of warmth wasn't included.

'You're not finishing your lunch?' Seth asked. 'Please yourself.'

'Lunch?' Clive said. 'Lunch? More like the bloody Last Supper.' He strode out of the restaurant angrily.

But driving into the mill yard with the chalk and peppermint taste of the antacid tablets holding off the bile but not the gnawing pain in his stomach, his anger was replaced by weariness. He had his reproaches ready for Donald; it was an unendurable situation. He had been betrayed by his own flesh and blood; the way that they'd run the mill all these years had been knocked askew. No matter how haphazard it might have seemed, Lendrick and Sons had survived and bigger firms with the benefit of business efficiency experts and whiz-kids from the City had gone under. And the shareholders had been happy. He'd played it by ear, Donald worked by the book: they were a team. And now it was spoiled, he didn't know where he was and he felt for the first time in his life that he was heading for a duodenal ulcer.

He had it in his mind to storm into the office, to thump the desk, to tongue-lash Donald; but he found himself entering quietly with scarcely the energy to pick up his feet. He certainly wasn't frightened, but he was overwhelmingly tired.

Donald didn't look up from his desk as Clive entered. Clive sat down on the sofa. 'I've seen Seth and Diana.'

Donald brought his head up slowly. 'Did anything useful emerge?'

151

'I think you're about to sell me down the river.'

'That's a damned silly way to put it.' Donald lit one of the cheroots he'd taken to recently.

'Do you know what'll happen if Bruce and that lot have their way?'

'You tell me. He's a shareholder. Seth's a shareholder. And a director. Diana's a shareholder. Maybe they should have their way.'

'Don't you approve of the French deal? I thought that you did.'

Donald frowned down at a letter and scribbled briefly in the margin. 'I'm rather busy, Clive. The answer is that the French deal isn't finalized.'

'No,' Clive said. He tasted bile again, though the pain in his stomach had gone. 'It isn't. You're a Byzantine bugger, aren't you?'

Donald smiled. 'I take it you don't mean that as a compliment.'

'Simply expressing my bewilderment.' Clive rose. 'We'll talk again, won't we?'

Donald didn't answer. Clive walked to the door. The reproaches were still all there, he was ready and willing to take the hide off Donald in bleeding tripe, to leave him crawling and utterly contrite; but he hadn't the energy. He had the cat-o'-nine-tails in his hand, he didn't feel any pity for Donald, he knew that the punishment would be justified. But his strength had all leaked away.

It was twenty minutes after Clive had returned to Lendrick Mills in Charbury that Ruth in the bookshop six miles north-east of Charbury began to recognize the tall slim woman staring at her from the other side of the counter. It didn't seem that the woman recognized her: her narrow pale face with the big mouth carelessly painted in too bright a red wore the expression of someone who'd been transported instantaneously to another planet. There was horror and fear in the vivid blue eyes, as if the bookshop were vast and crystalline, echoing with atonal music – high notes rising unendurably prolonged – colours changing into colours beyond the spectrum, menacing shapes circling her: she looked at Ruth as if she were the most menacing shape of all, the unbelievable and the implacable and the all-powerful and the totally inhuman. Her eyes weren't mad, Ruth thought: what they saw was real. But it wasn't what Ruth saw, it wasn't what anyone else in the shop saw.

'Ruth,' the woman said. 'Ruth Inglewood. You remember me.' The vivid blue eyes now were seeing the bookshop and the books and the High Street outside, but only with an effort. 'We met at a party. You had a gold lamé trouser suit.'

'Vicky Kelvedon.' Ruth smiled. 'Nice to see you. You haven't been around lately.'

'No,' Vicky said. 'That is absolutely the right way to put it. Not lately. Quite recently I've been around. But really I haven't been around anywhere . . . I'm clearing up now.' She put her hand on the counter. It was well-shaped but very thin, almost claw-like: her gold bracelet-watch fitted very loosely, seeming in danger of slipping off it as she put it on the counter. There were dark circles under her eyes. Her plum-coloured highwayman's cape had in itself enormous panache, but seemed to weigh her down; remembering her as once she'd know her, Ruth saw that something had departed from her.

'You're selling your house?' she asked.

'I might as well. I'm not all that keen on it here anyway –' She swayed a little. 'Christ!' she said. 'Sorry, something I ate, –'

Ruth came over and took her arm. It seemed childishly thin. 'Come and sit down,' she said.

'I'm sorry. I'm so sorry. I really am sorry – ' Vicky's eyes were wet. 'Didn't want to cause you trouble – '

'It's all right, love,' Ruth said gently, and took her into the office where Norman, with a grumpy expression, was ruffling through a pile of bills.

'Vicky darling!' He seemed pleased to put the bills aside.

'Look after the shop, Norman, will you? Vicky's not very well.'

'Of course, of course.' He flashed a quick smile at Vicky. 'You're in good hands, my dear. Where on earth have you been?' There was no real kindness in his voice.

Vicky looked at him dully and slumped into a chair. The slump was of complete fatigue, her legs splayed out bonelessly like a rag doll's.

'Can't I do something?' Ruth asked.

Vicky shook her head. 'It'll pass. I am sorry, I really am –' She took out a handkerchief and dabbed at her eyes with it.

Ruth put her arm round the thin shoulders. 'Would you like some coffee? Or whatever? You just have to ask.'

'Coffee,' Vicky said. 'Please. I'm just a bit – off it. Feeling my age.' She looked at Ruth. 'You don't change.'

'Perhaps I should.' Ruth plugged in the electric kettle and measured out Nescafé. 'I seem to have remained in this part of the world much longer than I intended.'

'I didn't intend to come to Hailton in the first instance. Bruce was moved here.' Vicky took out a packet of cigarettes and offered one to Ruth, who shook her head. 'I liked it best where we lived when we were first married. In Oxford. But I can't go back there. I can't go back anywhere.' She put her cigarette down and chewed her thumb. 'I'm not sure where I'm going to go.'

'Somewhere new,' Ruth said. 'I'd like that myself sometimes.'

'I feel like a ghost,' Vicky said. Her eyes were dry now; they looked larger and bluer than ever. 'Not really solid. I see Angus and Keith sometimes. My sons, you know. They're very polite. But I don't think they're mine any more.' She paused. 'How's Clive?'

'He's as happy as ever he was. He bends to the wind and doesn't break.' She poured out the coffee. 'Help yourself to sugar and milk.'

'You're better for him than ever I would have been.' Vicky drank her coffee greedily, holding the cup with both hands; colour came to her cheeks. 'I bend to the wind and I break. Jesus, I really do break. Break to bloody pieces.'

'Don't talk like that,' Ruth said. 'You're here, aren't you? You're alive – '

'Dried out,' Vicky said. 'Alive and dried out. It was a very good nursing home.' She paused and took a bottle of green tablets from her handbag.

'You don't have to tell me all this,' Ruth said. She looked at her watch.

'Don't worry, love, I'm going,' Vicky said. She squeezed Ruth's hand. 'Thanks for the coffee.'

'It's nothing,' Ruth said. 'Are you sure I can't do something for you? I could phone for a taxi – '

'I'm all right now. I'm seeing my lawyer, anyway. All sorts of arrangements are being made. Bruce is tidying up.' She grimaced. 'You know what's being tidied up? Me. Just me.'

'You're starting a new life,' Ruth said briskly. 'That's what matters. Nothing else.'

'Starting? I've already started it. It's not much improvement on the old one.' She stood up. 'Remember me to Clive.'

Ruth went with her to the door and out into the shop. 'Of course I will.'

'I'm not any bother to anyone now,' Vicky said. 'I'm being tidied away.' She kissed Ruth on the cheek and went out into the street, her eyes moist again. Norman, at the counter, smiled at her but she didn't seem to see him. Ruth stood gazing into the street after her; Norman put his hand on her arm.

'Darling, do you mind if I get back to those dreary old bills? Otherwise, we'll almost certainly be robbed blind.' His tone was waspish. 'What on earth's she after, anyway?' He lowered his voice. 'Got her eye on Clive again?'

'That's over,' Ruth said. 'A long time ago.' It was warm in the bookshop and a bright spring day outside, but for a split second she was in Vicky's shoes, no longer flesh and blood.

'She looks in a mess,' Norman said. 'Used to be quite lively.'

'They haven't left much of her,' Ruth said, half to herself.

'What's that?' Norman asked, already turning back to the office.

'It's of no consequence,' Ruth said. 'Go back to your bills, love.' She took the Concise Oxford Dictionary from the tousle-haired young man in blue jeans, who was now, she noted, becoming their best customer, put on her *Privileged to serve you and please come again* smile, wrapped up the book and took payment automatically, not able to get the words out of her mind. *They have not left much of Your Honour and me.* It was a long time since she'd read *Darkness at Noon*. The old peasant had said the words to Rubashov, looking at him with his sly peasant's smile. They must have been walking together round the prison yard.

It was a very moving passage: it meant that the old peasant was done for and he knew it. The words had enormous dignity. And it was the same with Vicky. There wasn't much left of her and she knew it. She deserved respect. But Ruth was glad to see the back of her: let the dead bury their dead, let the ghosts live amongst ghosts. She, Ruth, saw the May sun and welcomed the warmth and what she grasped she'd hold on to. And they – whoever they were – hadn't been able to destroy her. Because not so long ago and without telling anyone she'd said *To hell with it*. So she wasn't ever going to be a ghost or a prisoner. She wasn't ever going to be alone.

When the young man had gone she sat down behind the desk and folded her hands in her lap. She was still smiling. But it wasn't a shopkeeper's smile now; it was a spontaneous expression of pure animal contentment.

And she remained in that state of pure animal contentment until six-fifteen that evening at the White Rose, listening without much interest to Clive's account of his lunch at

Ferrand's Chophouse and finding increasingly distasteful his almost childish tone of complaint. When he went on to grumble about Donald she cut him off sharply.

'Darling, you're crying before you're hurt.'

'Christ, I thought you'd care.' Clive's face reddened. 'Can't you see they're ganging up on me?'

'It doesn't surprise me. Of course they're ganging up on you. I'm only surprised it hasn't happened before. It's simply that they don't like you; Donald, in particular, doesn't like you.'

'What on earth do you mean?' Now he was a spoilt little boy.

'A lot of people don't like you, darling. You're better than them, that's all.' Her eyes – sea-green, blue-green, he thought with pleasure for the thousandth and as if for the first time – were now compassionate. 'The ducks don't hate the ugly ducklings. They hate the swan.'

'Goddamn it, that doesn't make sense. Why should they hate me? What harm have I ever done them?' He was even more the spoilt little boy.

She put his hand quickly to her breast. 'You've never understood that, Clive, have you?' She put her hand down. 'That's why I love you.'

The brandy was settling his stomach and now at long last he'd got used to the new blue and green carpet and the new cork panels and the new red plush – the place had been run in, so to speak, he felt settled there, it wouldn't be long before the newness would all have been rubbed off. 'I love you, too,' he said. 'Not that I know what you're driving at.'

'It's of no consequence.' She lit a cigarette, inhaled, then stubbed it out. 'I should have told you: Vicky Kelvedon came in today.'

'Oh.' He stared at her, not certain what she expected his reaction to be. 'I thought she'd gone away?'

'Not yet. She wishes to be remembered to you.'

'How is she?' His tone was neutral: he couldn't help feeling that whatever he said was bound to be wrong.

'Not gloriously happy. Lost, in fact. Terribly thin. Dried out. Yes, dried out.'

'It's all over,' he said. 'A long time ago.'

'I know. She's not still carrying a torch for you. Or for anyone. She should be so lucky.'

Clive had a vision of Vicky two years ago, outrageous and impudent and not giving a curse, lifting him up at a time when he was down on his knees; he hadn't thought of her since that morning he'd left their flat in Charbury but now he liked thinking of her, she was a tune to dance to and a flower which would not fade. 'I'm sorry,' he said. 'I'd have liked her to be happy . . . I don't mean – ' He stopped.

'All right, darling. I wouldn't want you not to care.' She squeezed his hand. 'You're a good man. You don't really know how to be unkind, do you?'

He smiled. 'Don't I? Just give me half a chance.' He sighed. 'If only things would settle down a bit. I could cope. Everything changes.' He sipped his brandy. 'Except you . . . that's what keeps me going.'

'You think I'll always be the same person? The one who keeps you going?' She was now coldly angry. 'Yes, that's how you see me. Good old reliable Ruth. A nice undemanding mistress and a bosom for you to cry on. Someone who'll never cause you trouble – '

'Oh Christ, lay off me! What the hell's got into you? What on earth have I done wrong? What do I ever do wrong to you?' Again there was a note of self-pity in his voice.

'Stop being so defensive,' she said wearily. Her anger had gone now. 'I didn't say you'd done anything wrong.'

'Is it seeing Vicky that's done it? I told you, it's all over –'

'Of course it's not Vicky.' She smiled. 'Absolutely not. I'm going to have a baby.'

'Going to have a baby? God, what a mess! This on top of everything – ' He stopped. 'I'm sorry. Came as a shock. Are you sure?'

'Of course I'm sure. It was confirmed this morning.'

'Silly thing for me to say. Chaps always say it.' He put his hand on hers. 'Are you happy?'

'I'm happy,' she said. 'Are you?'

'Yes,' he said. 'Yes. It's quite good for my morale to be a father again. I'll do everything. I'll look after you. I really will –' He stopped as if fighting for breath, then recovered. 'Look, darling, you know I'll marry you.'

She shook her head. 'I'm glad to have had the offer, but that's not what I want.'

'Tell me what you do want.'

'I have it all,' she said. 'I don't need anything more.'

And now the feeling of pure animal contentment had taken over again and her words were the literal truth.

Thirteen

Unlocking the front door of Tower House forty-five minutes later, Clive knew what awaited him. It was nothing which he hadn't experienced before and at this stage in life nothing extraordinary. And yet he wanted to stay outside in the garden in the evening sunshine, wanted to be in an area where other voices could be heard, where cars would come to a stop and there'd be the sound of footsteps, where doors would close, meaning people had entered, where birds could be heard and, if one listened attentively enough, insects. It was children's voices which he liked hearing best: they stopped Chipfield Close from being too damned quiet.

Pausing at the door he reflected that though there were something like twenty young children in Chipfield Close and always, so it seemed, babies on the way, one didn't seem these days to see many of them around. Once, it had seemed, there were more people outside, walking down the road, using both front and back gardens, using and enjoying all the land which was, after all, what they'd paid quite a lot for. He thought of sitting outside for a moment on one of the garden benches, then decided against it. It would have looked a little eccentric, though once it would not have done. More and more, he felt vaguely, people were withdrawing, pulling up their draw-bridges. He sighed and went inside to an empty house, making straight for the study, the drinks table and the sofa. Lying on the sofa, his jacket and tie and shoes off, he let go, gave in, as the doctor after his heart attack had counselled him. Robin had left a beef casserole to be heated up for his supper; he considered whether to take a glass of wine with it, then decided against it. He didn't want it. There were more and more things which he didn't want. But Ruth was what he did want and he had understood her words. What he found disturbing was the question of whether she wanted him.

He found himself missing Petronella. It wasn't as it had been between them, she was for most of the time a stranger. Still, with daughters there always were moments when one could let down all one's defences, be stumbling and hurt and confused and their reactions would be warm and uncomplicated and immediate; there wouldn't be any cool appraisals of the situation or any sort of judgement, but simply love. A daughter's face was always a private face. His sons, George and Roger, had never given him any trouble, he was pretty certain they'd be high-flyers and certainly they'd never lacked respect for him. But he was more and more certain that their faces were always public faces – they'd never freak out, but he'd get no spontaneous hugs from them either.

Ruth was going to have a baby: a picture came into his mind which Petronella, despite her youth, could have valuated properly but which George and Roger couldn't. If he told them they'd take it in their stride as men of the world, there might even be a certain amount of all-boys-together, there's-life-in-the-old-dog-yet camaraderie. But Petronella would understand that a new life would be reinforcements and more than reinforcements. There'd be more people on his side. He hadn't been able to say this at the White Rose, he'd let Ruth down. For he'd only been able to see Seth and Diana ganging up on him and to sense that bastard Bruce Kelvedon in the background. Bruce was the barbarian hordes at the frontier and Donald was the trusted commander who would let the hordes pour in. If Donald had still been on his side, he wouldn't have been frightened: he knew who Donald's friends were and he knew the voting structure. But now it was a new game and he didn't know the rules. Before his heart attack he'd been able to keep any amount of balls in the air at once: now he could handle only one thing at a time.

A civilized arrangement with a civilized person, *cinq à sept* once a week with a woman who expressly didn't want marriage was an arrangement which could be left to run itself. There'd still be quiet evenings here with Robin, they'd still entertain here and be entertained, she'd still give him full support as a wife and be companionable too. And Petronella could for all they cared fill the house with her friends as long as they didn't break up the furniture and fittings. Ruth was only herself, she belonged to herself, she asked him for nothing but, when he came to think of it, his friendship. They were friends even before they were lovers. Robin was not his friend and had never been his friend. She was his wife. And Ruth had made it clear a thousand times that she was content as she was, that the amount of togetherness they had was as much as she wanted, that her home was a sovereign independent kingdom.

And now it wasn't going to be the same. He didn't expect her to ask him to make an honest woman of her or even to ask him for money: that wasn't her style. He didn't in fact give a damn what she asked for: it was his child and he'd maintain it. But for two years now he'd known precisely where he was and where he was going, he'd been able to keep all the balls in the air with ease and grace and a proper enjoyment. And now he was alone in an empty house and his act had been changed behind his back.

He yawned and closed his eyes, then got up abruptly, went to the phone and dialled a number.

'Clive Lendrick speaking,' he said. 'Bruce?'

'Nice to hear your voice, old chap.' There was a hint of a sneer in Bruce's voice.

'What the hell are you playing at?'

'Oh, you've seen Seth and Diana. I hope it was a constructive meeting.' The gloating note was unmistakable: Clive took a deep breath.

'It depends upon what you call constructive. I'd say that you were trying to put a spanner in the works.'

163

'Merely protecting our interests as shareholders, old chap.' The *old chap* set Clive's teeth on edge; Bruce just hadn't the accent to use it in the casual way it should be used: it was as if he were wearing an old school tie he wasn't entitled to.

'You should have been there then.'

'Too busy, I'm afraid. Anyway, I prefer to keep a low profile . . . By the way, old chap, Tracy is a shareholder as much as I am.'

'Taken as read, Bruce. Incidentally, I've seen Donald too.'

'I do hope that you didn't cause a scene.' Bruce chuckled. 'You know what that does to his stomach.'

'*His* stomach seems to be in good shape,' Clive said coldly. 'It's mine that worries me.'

'Sorry to hear that.' He didn't sound in the least sorry. 'You *do* sound unlike your usual unruffled self . . . ' He chuckled again.

'I've a bloody good right to be. I've a notion that somehow or other you're planning to mess up the French deal.'

'Really, Clive, you're talking through your hat. I'm not on the Board, to begin with. Though as a shareholder I'm entitled to my opinions. One of which is that Donald should have a bigger say. And that's for starters.'

'For starters. I think you have him by the balls.'

'Do we? He seems very happy about it. Maybe being properly valued makes all the difference.'

'You don't know anything about him. Or about the worsted trade.'

'Don't I? I know something about sound business administration, though. And have you forgotten about Seth?'

'Seth's just amusing himself. What the hell does it matter to him if Lendrick's goes down the Swanee? His Board's happy to have the silly old bugger out of the way.'

'You do have a pithy way of putting things, my dear Clive. But he's not the only one to feel discontented . . . ' He went on to give half a dozen names. 'Don't they know anything about the worsted trade, either? Is it only you?'

164

'All right. Let's stop arsing about. We'd better get together.'

'My plans are rather fluid – '

'Sod that!' He took out his pocket diary. 'Let's say next Wednesday. Eleven. At my office. And tell Seth and Diana.'

'Since it's all, in a sense, unofficial, I suggest my place,' Bruce said.

'My office,' Clive said firmly and hung up feeling more cheerful. Going into the kitchen to switch on the cooker he decided to have half a bottle of Burgundy after all. There was indeed life in the old dog yet, he thought, taking out the corkscrew from the Welsh dresser. Having opened the bottle he sat down at the table and poured himself a glass of wine. It didn't this time make him think of blood; he sipped it with relish, beginning now to realize how hungry he was. Robin had told him that she was visiting an old school friend, a widow in Skipton – it was a hen party for two, a girls' get-together, a gossip about old times since the old school friend was just passing through; he'd accepted it without question much as he'd accepted without question that Petronella was spending the night at the Villendams. There was no other way in which their lives could function: but for a moment he found himself regretting the time when the house wasn't so empty, when naturally they trusted each other but, of course, would ask questions. He frowned. It wasn't like that: there were no secrets.

And now he had a secret and it was a good secret too, though God knows it was the ultimate egg in the fan. And as he looked out into the sunlight he couldn't help feeling extraordinarily elated, not in the least tired, capable of taking on any amount of disgruntled shareholders. It was as if there weren't an empty room in the house, as if there were voices in every corner of it and every voice eager and young and alive.

Twenty-three miles away and six miles out of Skipton Robin and Stephen lay naked in bed together, absolutely still and scarcely breathing. There was no aggression on Stephen's face, but no defeat either. Tranquillity was an expression which sat well on Robin's face, but of late it had also been a protection from intruders, summoned up at some cost. Now it was tranquil as the country round the cottage was tranquil, as a rock is tranquil, as an animal is tranquil in its own territory. There was light through the dormer window and plenty of light: darkness was hours away. But it was a kind light, she felt, a light for lovers. And outside the small stone cottage the landscape was kind – hilly but not jagged, with plenty of trees for windbreaks, divided by zigzagging drystone walls. It wasn't rich, it wasn't lush, it wasn't in the least tame, it certainly would have thought it beneath its dignity to attempt any sort of charm, but it wasn't savage either.

There wasn't anything there that had to be kept out and nothing in the bedroom that had to be kept out. There was enough: a pine dresser, polished oak floorboards, two rush-bottomed chairs, a pine wardrobe, a sheepskin rug on either side of the double bed. It was, Stephen had remarked to her, oddly like his study at home in Weybridge: there was nothing superfluous but everything that was needed. She felt weightless now, and with the light came in quietness. It was quiet in Throstlehill but the city was still not so far away, the noise and the fumes and all the green covered over. From the narrow winding track beside the cottage one took the narrow winding road to Skipton and the castle and the market place where once as a child she'd seen a sheepdog sitting in the back of a big van. It was mostly black, with not an ounce of flab on it, very much alert, obeying its master's orders to stay put, doing its duty and absolutely content, as much a part of Skipton as the castle and part of the countryside too. She thought of that dog now and got the same enormous pleasure from thinking about it as she had the first time she'd come to the cottage with Stephen only a week ago.

'It's very good being here,' Stephen said, still not moving. 'Good – yes, that's it. Like Jesus going up into the mountains with His disciples and one of them saying *Master, this is a good place to be*.' He smiled. 'He got all excited and wanted to put up a memorial to Elijah or something.'

She put her hand on his chest. 'You're very hairy.' She rubbed his chest gently. 'Shall you be in Yorkshire again soon?'

'It's very likely. John Maltcomb seems likely to be about to make me an offer I can't refuse.'

'The one who lent you this cottage?' She recognized with a pang that, though not unhappy, he wasn't as tranquil as he had been.

'Who lent me it for his own purposes. Of course he wants me to be hired muscle for Deira, but he's also got a publishing project in mind. Based in Yorkshire.'

'Would you live here? Then I wouldn't have to wait three weeks to see you.'

'It's all in the air. But yes, I suppose I would. More or less.' He kissed her hand. 'You know, I never went much for this Man O'The Dales stuff before. But maybe this is the right place for me.'

'Maybe,' she said. 'Have you told Jean?'

'There isn't any need to yet.' He pulled the bedclothes down and kissed her breasts.

'We don't tell anyone anything, do we really?' she asked. 'It's funny – these last three weeks I've longed to tell someone. It would have made the waiting easier.'

'It wasn't an easy three weeks for me either. But don't tell anybody anything. They don't understand.' His mouth travelled to her belly and she drew in her breath as if in pain, then pushed the bedclothes down with her feet.

'You look more naked when you're naked than other women do,' he said. 'Why is that?'

'Stop talking,' she said, and pulled him down upon her.

At that moment twenty-nine miles away, Norman and Ruth at their flat in Charbury were finishing their supper of pork chops and roast potatoes. Ruth cleared her plate: Norman, normally rather greedy, hardly touched his food. But he drank more than his share of the wine; she left her glass half full.

'You're not yourself,' she said over coffee.

'Just a touch of the collywobbles, dear,' he said. 'No crisis. It's a bug going around . . . '

'Yes,' she said. 'But I don't like it when you don't eat. You're not going out then?'

'Not in my state of health, dear. There's nowhere I fancy going.' He lit another cigarette; he'd smoked throughout the meal and she noted with concern that his face tonight seemed even smaller, positively peaked. He wasn't smoking the cigarette; the cigarette was smoking him.

'You don't seem to see much of Gary these days,' she said.

'I'd rather not hear his name if you don't mind.'

She shrugged. 'It's none of my business.'

'We're friends,' he said. 'I shouldn't have snapped at you. Of course I'm not seeing much of Gary. He's seeing someone else.'

'I don't like seeing you unhappy,' she said gently.

'You're a good girl,' he said. He poured himself a stiff brandy. 'But what can't be cured must be endured.'

She smiled. 'That's rather bleak, isn't it?'

He seemed not to have heard her. 'It all happens from outside,' he said, half to himself. 'Like locusts, like a plague –'

She walked over to his chair, knelt beside him and took his hand. It was very cold. 'Cheer up, Norman darling. You'll be all right. I'm with you.'

'I won't be all right,' he said. 'But you will be, pet. Always, I can see that.' He looked at her with penetrating shrewdness.

'I don't have any secrets from you, do I?' she asked. She took his other hand. 'God, your hands are cold.' She began to rub them both: he let himself relax, the cigarette smouldering in the ashtray, the brandy unregarded.

Fourteen

Clive's meeting with the cabal – for that is how he'd come to think of Bruce, Tracy, Seth, Diana and Donald – didn't in fact take place on the Wednesday of the week after the Ferrand's Chophouse luncheon, but a week later: always at the last moment one of the cabal would phone to say they couldn't make it. In the case of Diana her secretary phoned: she said nothing he could positively complain about, but her manner indicated that he wasn't the sort of person with whom her employer should do business.

In short, as he told Ruth that evening in her flat just before supper, he felt at a disadvantage even before the meeting began.

'It wasn't a discussion,' he said to her, taking a gulp of Scotch. 'Equals have discussions. The buggers were giving me my orders.'

She arched her eyebrows. 'They can't do that, surely?'

'Technically they can't. But if they can swing the voting their way at the AGM, then it's a different matter.' He lifted his glass to his lips again, then put it down: he'd taken the first gulp too eagerly, he'd needed it too much. 'Bloody Donald's the nigger in the woodpile. If one dare use the phrase these days.'

'Why can't you have it out with him?'

'Do you think I haven't tried? I can't change him. He's too greedy for profits.' He looked round the untidy room for once without pleasure; it had been a dull and wet day, uncomfortably muggy: he had a curious feeling of being trapped, a middle-aged failure. Sourly he noted that a pile of books on the floor near his armchair was stacked haphazardly with some smaller books underneath: he would have stacked them in a sort of pyramid, the books decreasing upwards in size.

'I'd always thought that to be the whole purpose of the business,' Ruth said drily.

'Of course we've got to make profits. But not Donald's way. Christ, the ideas he came up with this morning! Thicker yarns is the latest – the cloth would still be Super Seventies, but it'd be a damned sight cheaper to make. And he wants to use a cheaper finish for the home market because in this country dye doesn't have to stand up to strong sunlight. Anything for a bigger profit. My father would turn in his grave!'

'I had the impression that you and he got on quite well together.' Ruth sounded impatient.

'Donald's head is stuffed with daft notions, but up till recently he hasn't seriously expected anything to be done about them. Now he does. And bloody Bruce is egging him on. So are Seth and Diana.'

'Why don't you let them get on with it?'

He stared at her. 'What? Take a back seat permanently? Let them ruin the business? Because they will. Worsted manufacture isn't high technology. That's what they all forget. You play it by ear and by instinct, you mustn't get too big. Donald's good at keeping things running. I'm good at selling and making decisions – '

'You could resign,' she said, even more impatiently. 'You've got enough to live on. Are you trying to be the richest man in the graveyard?'

'If I resigned, what would I do with myself?'

'That was no problem when you left Robin. I remember you were quite happy.'

He was silent for a moment. 'It's no good. I couldn't do that again.'

She flushed. 'You want to go on just as you are, don't you?'

'Forget it, I'm too tired. What's more on my mind is what we're going to do about the baby.'

'I was getting tired of hearing about Lendrick Mills. I'm glad you got round to the baby.'

'For Christ's sake, Ruth, you bite my head off every time I try to talk about it.'

'That doesn't mean you're not to talk about it. You should *want* to talk about it.'

He ran his hand through his hair. 'You can't win,' he muttered. 'You can't win.'

'I'm going away.' Her voice was calm now.

'Going away? This is a bit sudden. You mean just for a break?' He smiled. 'Not a bad idea. I think I'll come with you.'

'I'm going alone. I may not come back.'

'May not come back? But why are you going? There must be a reason.'

'If you don't know, I won't tell you.'

'What about Norman? What about the shop? What about this flat? You can't just walk out – '

'Everything's taken care of.' She smiled faintly. 'I'm not just a booksy girl, you know. We're getting another assistant, and all the details have been attended to. No problem, really. What would happen if I were ill? These things are very simple to arrange really . . . '

He stood up and then went across the room to her chair. 'I asked you to marry me.' He put his hands on her shoulders.

'I told you I wouldn't,' she said. 'But then I'm not all that struck on marriage. I told you that at the beginning. Don't you remember?'

He took his hands away from her shoulders. 'Darling, what do you want?'

'Maybe to find out who I am,' she said. 'Which is quite a tall order. But I've got to find out for myself. I'm not going to have anyone else tell me. Not even you.'

He went back to his chair. 'I can't understand,' he said, 'where you are going.'

'My parents' address will always find me.' She stood up. 'We'd better eat.'

'But when are you going? And just where? You must be going somewhere.

'I'm going tomorrow,' she said. 'You can easily enough find out where I'm going. If you really want to.'

'Of course I want to!' he shouted. 'You tell me how.'

'It's a small country,' she said. 'It'll be no trouble. I won't be in disguise. You'll know me when you see me, won't you?' Her tone was softer now, almost a plea for help.

Arriving at Tower House later that night he met Olive Villendam and her sister Elizabeth in the entrance hall on their way out. It was the briefest of encounters – smiles and a gesture of greeting – but it left him uplifted. The Villendam sisters were slim and bold-eyed, Olive dark and Elizabeth fair, feminine even in jeans and baggy T-shirts, and when he came into the house their voices transformed it, for a moment there was in his nostrils a scent of youth and unlimited tomorrows.

Robin was sitting at the desk writing when he came into the study. She looked at him as if at a stranger. 'I think we ought to have a talk.'

'We'll talk,' he said. 'But not for long. I'm tired.' He sat down, considered having a stiff whisky then decided against it. The rain was now beating hard against the windows: it didn't seem like May.

Robin ripped off a sheet from her writing-pad, crumpled it into a ball and dropped it into the wastepaper basket under the desk. She stood up and crossed to the chair opposite him. 'I've been to the Players. I saw Norman.'

He yawned. 'Did you? Well, as the saying goes, no show without Punch.'

'Norman told me a secret. About Ruth being pregnant.'

He laughed. 'It's not going to be a secret for very long, is it?'

'He made the most of it,' she said bitterly. 'Yes, he really did. He really did want to hurt me.'

'People like Norman always have a nasty streak. Though he's better than most.'

'Is he indeed?' Her face for a moment turned shrewish. 'Well, you're the expert. You've lived under the same roof with him.'

'Take it easy, Robin. Take it very easy.' He found himself ragingly angry. 'I was sleeping with Ruth, not bloody Norman.'

'All right, I'm sorry. But why didn't you tell me?'

'I haven't known all that long. Scarcely a fortnight. It was more than I could handle. Too much is happening . . .' From outside he could hear above the sound of the rain water splashing from the guttering. 'Did Norman tell you Ruth was going away?'

She raised her eyebrows. 'He didn't tell me that. It's no skin off my nose. But it does make a difference to you. Yes, I can see that.' She looked at him with a cool pity which he found himself resenting. 'What are you going to do, Clive? Yes, it changes things. You did have a very nice routine. Better really than I've had.' Now she seemed to be almost gloating.

'Don't push it,' he said. 'Don't push it. Don't ask me any more questions.'

'Don't ask me any questions now either,' she said.

'You're seeing Stephen again,' he said. 'That's not a question. It's a statement.'

'Yes. Leave it at that.' She got up. 'Sure you don't want a hot drink?'

'I'll have some Horlick's.'

'I think I'll just have hot milk myself,' she said with great deliberation. She stood still for a moment, looking at him intently. 'I'll tell you something, Clive. She's got what I'll never have. I can't give Stephen a child, can I? *I'll never forgive her that. Never.*' Her face went white and she hissed out the last words.

'I can't answer that,' he said. He rose with an effort; there was nothing wrong with his legs, but messages from his brain to his muscles were being delayed. He walked out of the room very slowly and stiffly, as if he had to think out each step.

Climbing the stairs he had to use the handrail and found it difficult to breathe; he needed to stop to rest, but had a sense of being pursued. He didn't recognize the woman he'd just been with as Robin, and he didn't recognize the woman he'd been with earlier as Ruth. Throwing his clothes off in his room, he collapsed into bed: he got his pyjamas on, feeling it somehow important, but hadn't the energy to button the jacket. The sheets were cool; outside it was still raining heavily. He felt a strange detachment: events were about to take over. Why was it that there'd been changes at the last moment and he hadn't been informed?

He was considering this with no sense of urgency and without feeling the need for any kind of rationalization when Robin came in with a mug and a plate of biscuits on a tray. She put them down on the bedside table. She sat down at the foot of the bed.

'I'm going away, Clive.'

'Join the fucking club,' he said with a spasm of anger. 'When?'

'Soon. Stephen's got a cottage near Skipton.'

'I thought it was going to be Hailton.' He took a sip from the mug and found himself enjoying it.

'That was never really on. It's always been OK for you to have Ruth in Charbury, though. Hasn't it?'

'I don't have anyone now.' He took another sip. 'Where the hell is your demon lover, anyway?'

'I'm not here to be cross-examined,' she said coldly.

'Is he leaving his wife then?' Suddenly he was very tired.

'Somehow I don't think so.' She picked up his suit and tie and put them away in the wardrobe. Picking up his shirt and underwear and socks, she clutched them to her. 'It doesn't really matter what he does.'

'Whatever he does won't make you any happier. As anyone else. From the little I know of him, the bugger's selfish to the core.' He made the statement without rancour.

'You're quite right, dear,' she said in a dead voice. She

looked down at his shirt and socks and underwear. 'I'll put these in the laundry basket.'

'What about Petronella?' he asked.

'Everything will be attended to,' she said. She went to the door.

He lay back on his pillow with a sense of relief. He had nothing against her, but he wanted to be alone. He was certain of nothing any longer except that he liked the taste of the Horlick's and the coolness of the clean sheets and the sound of the rain.

He rose, showered, shaved and dressed in the morning and went to the mills as usual. But in a sense he didn't wake up until fifteen days later, sitting in the White Rose with Norman. It wasn't that in any way he was unbalanced and, though far from happy, wasn't deeply distressed. He didn't like what had happened, but it had all happened to other people and wasn't in the least extraordinary. Other men's wives and mistresses left them, and other men came home to an empty house. And other men at a board meeting suddenly found themselves outvoted and deals like the French deal deferred for further consideration, which meant that the deal was off. It wasn't that he'd doubted the reality of what had happened: a dream is real enough when one's in it. But in a dream one is helpless, one merely suffers, and now listening to Norman with what he hoped was a sympathetic expression, he wasn't helpless and he wasn't going to suffer; it was seven o'clock on a fine June evening and he was no longer asleep.

'He was so damned offhand.' Norman was on the verge of tears. 'So callous, so *perfunctory*.' He sniffed. 'After all I've done for that boy . . . She said if he didn't give me my marching orders she wouldn't lend him the money he wanted . . . He's been *bought*. Yes, *bought* . . .'

'People who can be bought aren't worth having. You're well shot of him, Norman.' He recognized the real anguish in the voice which of late seemed to have become even more mannered.

'It's easy to say that,' Norman said. He blew his nose loudly. 'You don't have to tell me how horrible he is. That's nothing to do with love.'

'I'm not ignorant of such things,' Clive said gently.

'You know more than most people,' Norman said. 'But that's not saying much.' He took out a box of Balkan Sobranie Cocktail cigarettes, selected a mauve one and lit it. It was his sixth since they'd come in at half-past five. 'Have you heard from Ruth?'

Clive shook his head. 'I told you.' He got up. 'I've got to make a phone call, Norman. See you.'

'I hope you will,' Norman said. 'I hope you will.' He seemed on the verge of tears again.

Robin, at that moment in the cottage near Skipton, was eating dinner with Stephen. They hadn't been to bed. He'd been in Yorkshire since Monday and that day had had a particularly exhausting and protracted session at Deira TV, during which, though there'd been plenty to eat and drink available, he'd had to watch himself very carefully because, as he himself put it, this particular set of bastards would tear his throat out the moment he dropped his guard. He had, in short, come home tired after a long hard day at the office, and now after an aperitif of a bone-dry Martini he was enjoying lamb chops, spinach and potatoes duchesse and drinking Moët & Chandon, which she'd remembered in the nick of time he didn't like too dry. Afterwards there'd be fresh pineapple and cream. There wasn't any sense of hurry: this time she wouldn't leave a warm bed to go home. The cottage was home now and it was a home for two people. The room they were in – surprisingly spacious, with a low oak-beamed ceiling, dark oak furniture and a large open fireplace – was the only room she needed. The large Victorian sofa and the two wing-sided armchairs were comfortable and there was a walnut davenport if Stephen wanted to do any writing. There were no empty rooms, so there was no loneliness. The spare room didn't count because it was so tiny, for unexpected guests only.

Stephen put down his knife and fork. 'I enjoyed that,' he said. His face had been drawn when he came in, on the verge of twitching; now his colour had come back, he almost looked younger. He glanced through the window. 'God, I really do like it here. The heat's off. Even though they're wolves in human form at Deira, it's different in Yorkshire.'

'Do you think you'll spend more time here?'

'It's on the cards,' he said. 'I'm making friends all the time. Friends? Well, let's say they feel that I'm rapacious and cunning enough to be a useful member of their pack.'

'I wish you wouldn't talk like that,' she said sharply.

'It's to stop myself from weakening. You know the saying? It's a great life if you don't weaken.' He poured himself more champagne. 'Maybe I ought to weaken a bit.'

'Stay as you are,' she said. 'I've never asked you to change.'

He went over to her and kissed her on the mouth very lightly, then knelt down beside her, his hands on her thigh. 'I'd like to be here with you in the winter. There'd be snow and we could burn logs on the fire. It would be really quiet. Gentle and wonderful. Really serene . . . '

She put his hands upon her breasts. 'Don't go too far into the future – '

The phone range. 'Fuck it,' he said. He got up.

'Does Jean know where you are?'

He shook his head. 'Graham Sullow does. My *friend*. But what the hell would he want at this hour?'

'You'd better answer it,' she said.

He walked over to the phone with deliberate slowness. When he picked it up she saw his face change, become drawn again.

'Jean! What the hell's up? Is it Julian?' A nerve in his cheek was actually twitching now. 'Oh, all right then.' His body sagged. 'No, for Christ's sake! Are you bloody well drunk? I'm here on business. What? No, absolutely not.' There was a long pause: his body tautened. 'Go to hell!' He rang off.

'Blackmail,' he said and sat down scowling at the table. 'Home at high noon or else she takes off.' He took out a cheroot. 'What the hell has bloody Graham told her?'

'You'll go, of course,' she said.

He stared at her, his face flushed. 'And give her the whiphand over me? For the rest of my life?'

'She holds all the cards.' She pushed her chair back abruptly and got up. 'It's a fine night. You'll make it for high noon.' She half ran out of the room.

He looked at the closed door blankly, then shook himself like a dog emerging from water, went over to the phone and dialled.

'Graham? You cunt, what have you told her?' His voice was thick with anger. 'I said only in case of emergency. What? Don't give me that, you bloody pimp, you – ' He stopped, gasping for breath. 'What do I care if the old sod's died? You don't have to bury him yet, do you? Or has he already begun to stink? What's that again? Oh – ' His face changed. 'You'll have to wait and see. Sweat it out. I always said you were the poor man's Machiavelli.' He hung up, went to the table again and lit his cheroot.

With part of his mind he wanted to stay with Robin. He looked forward to winter and the snow falling softly and the logs blazing in the open fireplace. But with another part of his mind he was with increasing joy considering the fact that Graham Sullow hadn't split on him just out of a sense of mischief, that Number One had indeed come in, his time being up, and that Graham wanted him by his side at Saxon immediately. Graham would want him there for his own, Graham's, benefit naturally: but naturally, he'd be aware that he, Stephen, did nothing for nothing. He was smiling to himself now, no longer in the least angry, then picked up the phone again.

*

Clive, announcing his resignation in the library of Seth's big house in Burley-in-Wharfedale, was still grateful to be awake. During the last fifteen days, the bad days of the long dream, he'd been trying to hold on to power, trying to drum up support from every quarter, but never being certain of what form the support could take. Nothing was official, no minutes were being kept: no rules were broken because there were no rules about shareholders meeting privately to discuss the policy of Lendrick and Sons. And Donald could vote as he liked. That would have been his father's intention. Clive realized now that he'd been like a general of the old school fighting well-trained guerrillas. Now he'd retreat with his forces intact and the full honours of war.

He didn't put it this way, but within less than ten minutes made it clear that he was stepping down of his own accord, he was retiring undefeated. He felt very much at ease in the room: it was light and spacious with beech shelves and a large Persian rug on the parquet floor, and the books which filled two walls very emphatically hadn't been bought by the yard.

'This isn't a formal announcement,' he concluded. 'But by all means tell Bruce and Tracy.' He sipped his Scotch. 'And Donald.'

Seth, who had been listening impassively behind his large leather-topped desk, spoke for the first time. 'Haven't you told Donald?'

'I only decided this evening. It's entirely my decision.'

'Is it, by gum!' Seth puffed his cigar. 'You're going to take your bat home, is that it?'

Clive shrugged. 'That's one way of describing it. But it isn't my bat any more, is it?'

'That depends. You'd better tell him, Diana.'

'It may not come to you as a surpise but Bruce and Tracy are acting for someone else. Quillow-Perquita-Perelman Inc. and Associates.' She pulled down her skirt a little making him still more aware of her long slim legs in black lacy tights. Her face was even more than ever tonight that of a soubrette; he wrenched his eyes away from her, aware that she sensed his feelings.

'They take things over,' Seth said. 'Strangers in the town. From another country.'

'Does that matter? OK, they're asset-strippers in a big way. They're not the only ones. We have our native vultures.'

''We know how to deal with them.' Seth chuckled. 'At least we know how to get at the buggers.'

'They were trying to use us, you see,' Diana said. There was honest indignation in her voice.

Clive finished his Scotch. 'That would never do.' He was still wide awake, he wouldn't go back into the dream again. 'To attempt to manipulate two small investors like you and Seth – words fail me!'

'All right, Clive. Stop taking the mickey out of us. Just think again, that's all. Bruce and Tracy are out. That's what it amounts to. Just forget what you said about resigning.' His tone was wheedling now.

'Donald's still in a sticky position.'

'That can be rectified. The truth is, maybe we've all been a bit hasty. No harm in talking about it.'

'No harm at all,' Clive said. 'We'll have a nice long talk.' He poured himself another Scotch, still grateful to be awake. He looked at Diana's legs again. She saw the direction of his eyes and looked back at him amusedly.

Norman at that moment, newly bathed and shampooed, his skin tingling with cologne and soothed by talc, was stepping into freshly laundered blue pyjamas and red morocco slippers. He put on a blue silk polka-dot dressing-gown and red silk scarf and walked into the living-room. When Ruth had been there he'd always been making abortive attempts to tidy it: now that she'd gone he found himself no longer caring.

It was a fine evening and the sun was still bright, but he switched on the gas fire on the hearth. He didn't know why he did it, but somehow it gave him comfort. He walked around the room touching things for a moment, taking them up and putting them down for no particular purpose. He was not thinking of Gary; instead he kept thinking of Clive. He didn't fancy Clive and never had, he thought with irritation. Why did he keep seeing that agreeable face with the features a shade too large, why was he so fascinated by the fact that, even when it was stricken and bemused, it always had faith in itself?

He went into the bathroom, took out a bottle of pills from the wall cabinet, inspected his face in the mirror, smoothed his hair. Momentarily, he saw Gary's face. It went away when he returned to the living-room and switched on the record-player.

He lay on the studio couch, three cushions under his head, a bottle of brandy, a glass, the bottle of pills, a new box of Balkan Sobranie Cocktail cigarettes and his gold lighter on the coffee table beside him. He closed his eyes, listening to Noël Coward's clipped voice, but saw Clive's face again. He opened his eyes and selected a pink cigarette. When he'd finished the cigarette he took out four pills and washed them down with brandy. Another cigarette later – mauve this time – he fell asleep briefly, then he was fully awake, wondering dazedly what had kept Ruth. He was in a cold sweat now and the sweat smelled stronger than the Eau Sauvage. He poured himself more brandy and emptied the pills into a little heap on the table.

The last sound he heard was 'Some Day I'll Find You': he saw nothing but the empty untidy room. He was, when the song began, about to arrive at an absolutely satisfying explanation of his situation, had a picture in his mind of a chain of events, of the dog which chased the cat which worried the rat, of the cow with the crumpled horn and the maiden all forlorn, all in the house that Jack built. And soon he would understand why the house that Norman had built was falling down and was exhilarated by the knowledge: but there wasn't even time for him to hear the end of the song.

*

Robin was in the study when Clive and Diana came in. She'd made herself a pot of tea but had let it grow cold. Her hands were folded on her lap and she was breathing evenly. She was trying to see her sons George and Roger, actually to bring them into the room, but only saw them for the duration of a camera flash: there was darkness, an instantaneous vision of two tall fair-haired young men, then an even more complete darkness. They were very different in appearance: George's face was leaner, his features sharper, Roger was taller and his features on a different scale. But when seen for so short a time, they looked like identical twins.

Clive switched the light on when he came in: she shaded her eyes.

'You're home,' he said, walked over to her and kissed her. He waved in the direction of Diana. 'I think you've met Diana Keysham.'

'We met at the Spring Parade,' Robin said. She was aware that there wasn't any sort of welcome in her voice, but at that moment had simply wanted to go on sitting there alone.

'Do sit down, Diana,' Clive said rather fussily. Robin saw that his colour was too high. And he smelled of whisky.

'No thanks, Clive,' Diana said. 'I have to make an early start tomorrow.' She turned to Robin, a half-smile on her face. 'Seth and I have kept him out late on business, Mrs Lendrick. He's put us straight. He really has.' She held her hand up to Clive. 'No, I'll see myself out.'

'We'll have another long talk soon,' Clive said.

'I'll look forward to it. Good night. Good night, Mrs Lendrick.' She flashed them both a brisk smile and walked quickly out of the room.

'I'll see you,' Clive said. He sat down and yawned. Then he glanced at the teapot. 'Is there a cup there for me?' He yawned again.

'I'll make you some fresh.' She frowned at him. 'What's it with this Diana creature?'

He smiled rather complacently. 'Business. Purely business.

She's a shareholder and in the rag trade. She and Seth and I sorted out a few problems tonight. There was a slight emergency.'

'You'll have a few more problems with her.'

'Never mind that. It's just business, nothing else. She drove me home because I was tired and had had a drop too much whisky. What about you?' He looked at her anxiously. 'What's happened?'

'He's gone away. The same old story.' A nerve in her cheek was twitching.

'Will he come back?'

'No. No. This isn't his place. Even if he'd got the job he wanted here he wouldn't have stayed. He just doesn't belong here. And his wife has the child. It wasn't on from the start, you know. It really wasn't – ' She put her hand in her mouth and bit it as if to prevent herself from crying out.

'He's nothing but trouble. Doesn't make it any easier to bear, does it?'

She shook her head. 'I don't want him to come back.'

'We'll go away if you like. Or I'll go away – anything you want.' He went over to the sofa and sat beside her. 'We'll get through all this somehow. But these things pass – '

'Yes, so you've said before. I suppose they do.' She smiled at him. 'Don't worry. I'm home now. It's just the two of us and the storm has passed. That's what I tell myself.'

'Maybe things will settle down now.' His tone was momentarily peevish. 'Christ, all I've ever wanted is a quiet life.'

'A quiet life? You'll be lucky.' She went to the door. 'I'll make the tea.'